D1029807

BLACK ELVIS

FLANNERY
O'CONNOR
AWARD
FOR
SHORT
FICTION

Nancy Zafris,
Series Editor

BLACK ELVIS

STORIES BY GEOFFREY BECKER

THE UNIVERSITY OF GEORGIA PRESS ATHENS

Published by the University of Georgia Press

Athens, Georgia 30602

www.ugapress.org

© 2009 by Geoffrey Becker

All rights reserved

Designed by Mindy Basinger Hill

Set in 10.5 / 14.5 pt Minion Pro

Printed and bound by [TK]

The paper in this book meets the guidelines for
permanence and durability of the Committee on
Production Guidelines for Book Longevity of the
Council on Library Resources.

Printed in the United States of America

13 12 11 10 09 C 5 4 3 2 1

Library of Congress Cataloging-in-Publication Data

Becker, Geoffrey, 1959–

  Black Elvis : stories / by Geoffrey Becker.

      p.   cm. — (The Flannery O'Connor Award for short fiction)

  ISBN-13: 978-0-8203-3410-3 (cloth : alk. paper)

  ISBN-10: 0-8203-3410-3 (cloth : alk. paper)

  I. Title.

  PS3552.E2553B53 2009

  813'.54—dc22   2009016781

FOR NORA AND BRUNO

CONTENTS

ACKNOWLEDGMENTS

Grateful acknowledgment is made to the following publications, in which some of these stories first appeared in slightly different form: *The Cincinnati Review* ("This Is Not a Bar"); *Crazyhorse* ("Another Coyote Story"); *The Gettysburg Review* ("The Naked Man"); *New England Review* ("Black Days"); *Ploughshares* ("Black Elvis," "Iowa Winter," "Cowboy Honeymoon"); *Prairie Schooner* ("Jimi Hendrix, Bluegrass Star": reprinted from the *Prairie Schooner* 78, no. 1 [spring 2004] by permission of the University of Nebraska Press; copyright © 2004 by the University of Nebraska Press); *The Roanoke Review* ("Santorini"); *Shenandoah* ("Imaginary Tucson"); *Sonora Review* ("Know Your Saints"); *Third Coast* ("Man Under"). "Black Elvis" also appeared in *The Best American Short Stories 2000* (Mariner Books).

Thanks to the following people, who lent their own creative talents by providing editorial advice on one or more stories: Madison Smartt Bell, Jessica Anya Blau, Stephen Donadio, Michael Kimball, Steve Rinehart, Nora Sturges, and Ron Tanner. Big thanks, as well, to my copyeditor, Dorine Jennette, Series Editor Nancy Zafris, and to the excellent staff at the University of Georgia Press.

BLACK ELVIS

BLACK ELVIS

At 5:00 p.m. precisely, Black Elvis began to get ready. First, he laid out his clothes: the dark suit, the white dress shirt, the two-tone oxfords. In the bathroom, he used a depilatory powder to remove the stubble from his face, then carefully brushed his teeth and gargled with Lavoris. He applied a light coating of foundation, used a liner to deepen the effect of his eyes. They were big eyes, the color of old ivory, and examining them in the mirror, he had to remind himself once again whose they were.

At the bus stop, his guitar precariously stowed in a chipboard case held together by a bungee cord, he was watched by two shirtless boys on a stoop, drinking sodas. Their young, dark torsos emerged out of enormous dungarees like shoots sprouting.

"Yo," one of them called. "Let me see that."

Black Elvis stayed where he was but tightened his grip on the case. The boys stood and walked over to him. The sun hung low in the sky, turning the fronts of the row houses golden red.

"Are you a Muslim, brother?" asked the smaller of the two. His hair was cornrowed, and one eye peered unnaturally to the side.

Black Elvis shook his head. He wondered how hot it still was. Eighty, at least.

"He's a preacher," said the other one. "Look at him." This boy, though larger, gave the impression of being less sure of himself. His sneakers were untied and looked expensive and new.

"Singing for Jesus, is that right?"

"No," said Black Elvis.

"For who, then?" said the smaller one.

"For an audience, my man. I have a gig." He knew this boy. Sometimes he drew pictures on the sidewalk with colored chalk.

"Yeah?" The boy trained his one useful eye on the guitar case, the other apparently examining something three feet to the left. "Go on and play something then."

"I'm a professional. No professional going to play songs at no bus stop."

"When the bus come?"

Black Elvis examined his watch. "Any time now."

"You got time. Play us something."

"Was I talking to this here lamppost? Black Elvis don't play no bus stops."

"Black what?" said the bigger of the two boys.

"Elvis."

"Dude is tripping out."

"Yo, Black Elvis. Why don't you help us out with a couple of dollars? Me and my boy here, we need to get some things at the store."

He considered. He had bus fare and another eight dollars on top of that which he intended to use for beer at Slab's. In case of emergency, there was the ten-dollar bill in his shoe, under the Air-Pillo insole. He dug into his pocket and pulled out two ones.

"All right, then," he said, and handed them the money.

The smaller one leaned very close as he took it. He was about the same size as Black Elvis, and he smelled strongly of underarm.

"You crazier than shit, ain't you?"

"You take that two dollars," Black Elvis said calmly as the bus pulled in. "Go on over to Kroger's and get yourself some Right Guard."

At Slab's, the smell of grilled meat permeated the walls and the painted windows that advertised ribs, beer, and live music, and extended well out into the parking lot. The dinner rush had already started and there was a good-sized line of people waiting to place orders. A. J. was working the register, his grizzled white beard stubble standing out against his skin, grease flames shooting up from the grill behind him as slabs and half slabs were tossed onto the fire. If hell had a front desk, he looked like he was manning it.

Butch, who ran the blues jam, was at his usual front table, near the stage, finishing a plate of ribs, beans, and slaw. "Black Elvis," he said, with enthusiasm. He wiped his mouth with a napkin, then smoothed his goatee. His pink face glistened with a thin layer of sweat. "What is up?"

"Oh, you know, same old, same old. You got me?"

"I got you, man, don't worry." He tapped a legal pad with one thick finger. "Wouldn't be the blues jam without Black Elvis."

"I know that's right."

"You heard about Juanita?"

"No."

"Oh, man. She died last night. In her sleep. Put in her regular shift, just sassing people like she always did, you know. Didn't seem like anything was wrong with her at all. But I guess she had a bad ticker. She was a little overweight."

"She was, at that." He thought about Juanita's huge butt and breasts, how she more waddled than walked. But dead? How could that be?

"Yeah, it's a sad thing," said Butch. "Kind of makes you realize how fragile it all is, for all of us."

He watched as the drummer hauled the house snare drum out from the women's bathroom, where it was stored, up next to the stage. The wall behind the stage was painted to look like Stone Mountain, but instead of Confederate generals, the faces looking down at the crowd were those of B. B. King, Muddy Waters, Robert Johnson, and someone else who Black Elvis could never be quite sure about. Whoever had done the painting wasn't much of an artist.

"Hey, you want a beer?" Butch poured the remainder of the

pitcher on the table into what looked like a used glass. "Go on man, on the house."

Black Elvis picked up a napkin and ran it carefully around the rim of the glass. "Thanks," he said.

He found himself a seat next to a table of rich white folks who had been to some movie and were arguing about whether the actress in it had had her breasts enlarged. It had been a long time since Black Elvis had been to the movies, although he sometimes watched the ones they had running back in the video department of the Kroger's where he cut meat. They mostly looked the same to him, flickering postage stamps of color. They ought never to have gone to color, he thought. A picture ought to be in black and white. He remembered going to a picture with his father years ago that had pirates in it and Errol Flynn. His father wouldn't buy him popcorn, said it was a waste of money. He must have been about eight. The war was over. There were ships and sword fighting and men with long hair, and suddenly his daddy was pressing a hard-boiled egg into his hand and saying, "Go on, boy, take it." He ate the egg, shucking it carefully into his hand and placing the shells into the pocket of his shirt, while all around him he smelled the popcorn he really wanted.

He looked up. They'd asked him something, but he could not be sure what.

"Napkins?"

He pushed the dispenser toward them. He'd drifted someplace, it seemed. He took a swallow of beer. He needed something inside him, that was all—some weight to keep him from floating away. He was Black Elvis. He had a show to put on.

He'd been doing the jam now for four years. Everyone knew him. They relied on him. Sometimes he changed his repertoire around a little bit, threw in "I Can't Help Falling in Love" or something else unusual—he had a version of "You Were Always on My Mind," but it just never sounded right to him—but for the most part he was a

Sun Sessions man. "That's All Right," for an opener. "Good Rockin' Tonight." "Mystery Train." "Milkcow Blues." If there was a band, he was happy to play with them, but it didn't matter, he could do his songs by himself, too. He twisted his lip, stuck out his hip, winked at the ladies. Two years ago, *Creative Loafing* had done an article on Slab's and his picture appeared next to it, almost as if his face were an addition to the mural, and he kept this taped to the wall next to his bed.

There were moments he'd tucked away in his mind the way people keep photos in their wallets, ones that stood out from the succession of nights of cigarette and pork grease smell, of cold beers and loud music. The time he'd explained to a fine young blonde whose boyfriend had come down to show off his rock and roll guitar playing, that it was Elvis who had said "I'd rather see you dead little girl, than to be with another man," in "Baby, Let's Play House," and not The Beatles, and the way she'd looked at him then and said, "You mean they *stole* it?" and he smiled and said, "That's exactly what I mean." Or the time a young white man in a suit gave him a fifty-dollar tip and said "You're the best dang thing I've seen in this whole dang town, and I been here one year exactly come Friday."

He should have been the first one called. That was usual. That was the way things went on blues jam night. But that wasn't what happened. Instead, Butch played a few songs to open—"Let the Good Times Roll" and "Messin' with the Kid"—then stepped to the microphone and looked right past Black Elvis.

"We got a real treat here tonight," he said. "Let's all give it up for Mr. Robert Johnson. I'm serious, now, that's his real name. Give him a nice hand."

From somewhere in the back, a person in an old-fashioned-looking suit and fedora worked his way up through the crowded restaurant, holding a black guitar case up high in front of him. Trailing out from the back of the hat was a straight black ponytail. When he reached the stage he opened the case and took out an antique guitar. He turned around and settled into a chair, pulling the boom mike down and into place for himself to sing, while Butch arranged another mike for the instrument. Black Elvis just stared.

The man was Chinese.

"Glad to be here," said Robert Johnson. "I only been in Atlanta a week, but I can tell already I'm going to like it a lot." He grinned a big, friendly grin. His voice sounded southern. "Just moved here from Memphis," he said. "First thing I did, I said, 'Man, where am I gonna get me some decent ribs in this town?'" He plucked at the guitar, made a kind of waterfall of notes tumble out of it. "I can tell I'm going to be putting on some weight around here." There was laughter from the crowd.

Black Elvis drank some more beer and listened carefully as Robert Johnson began to play the Delta blues. He was good, this boy. Probably spent years listening to the original recordings, working them out note for note. Either that, or he had a book. Some of those books had it like that, exact translations. But that wasn't important. What was important was on the inside. You had to feel the music. That just didn't seem likely with a Chinese man, even one that came from Memphis.

He did "Terraplane Blues." He did "Sweet Home Chicago," and "Stones in My Pathway." He played "Love in Vain." Black Elvis felt something dark and opiate creeping through his blood, turning harder and colder as it did so. It should have been him up there, making the crowd love him. But the more he watched, the more he was convinced that he simply could not go on after Robert Johnson. With his pawnshop guitar and clumsy playing, he'd just look like a fool.

He watched Butch's face and saw the enjoyment there. He'd never seen the crowd at Slab's be so quiet or attentive to a performer. Robert Johnson *did* feel the music, even if he was Chinese. It was strange.

Black Elvis glanced toward the front door and wondered if there was any way at all he might slip unnoticed through the crowded tables and out.

When Robert Johnson finished his set, people applauded for what seemed like hours. He stood and bowed, antique guitar tucked under one arm. Black Elvis felt he was watching the future, and it was one that did not include him. But that was negative thinking. You couldn't let yourself fall into that. He'd seen it happen to other people his age, the shadows who walked around his neighborhood, vacant eyed, waiting to die. Esther, who lived in 2-c, just below him, who watched television with the volume all the way up and only opened the door once a week for the woman from Catholic Social Services to come deliver her groceries. That woman had stopped up to see Black Elvis, but he'd sent her away. Ain't no Catholic, he'd said. That's not really necessary, she told him. So he told her he carried his own groceries, and got a discount on them, too. Then he shut the door.

They were talking to him again, those people at the next table. He shook his head and wondered where he'd gone. His mind was like a bird these days.

"You're up," they told him. "They want you."

He brought his guitar up onto the stage. Robert Johnson had taken a seat with Butch, and they were talking intently about something. Butch had out a datebook and was writing in it. Butch booked the music for Slab's, on the other nights, the ones where the performers got paid. Robert Johnson's Chinese eyes squinted tight as pistachio nuts when he smiled.

"Black Elvis," someone shouted. He heard laughter.

"I'm going to do something a little different," he said into the microphone. "A good person passed last night. Some of you probably heard about it by now. Juanita—" he struggled to find her last name, then heard himself say "Williams," which he was certain was wrong, but was the only name he could come up with. "Juanita was, you know, family for us here at Slab's, and we loved her. So I'd like to dedicate this song to Juanita. This one's for you, baby."

He played a chord and was not surprised when his fourth string snapped like an angry snake striking. Ignoring this, he began to sing.

"Amazing grace, how sweet the sound . . ."

He didn't know if the next chord should be the same, or different, so he just played E again. It wasn't right, but it wasn't that wrong.

"That saved a wretch like me . . ."

He remembered his mother singing this. He could see her on the porch, stroking his sister Mae's head, sitting in the red metal chair with the flaking paint, the smell of chicken cooking in the kitchen flowing out through the patched window screen. His own voice sounded to him like something he was hearing at a great distance.

"I once was lost, but now I'm found . . ."

The people were staring at him. Even A. J. had stopped ringing up sales and was watching, the fires continuing to dance behind him.

"Was blind, but now I see."

He lowered his head and hit a few more chords. He felt like he was in church, leading a congregation. He looked up, then nodded somberly and went back to his chair.

"That was beautiful, man," said Butch, coming over to him. "Just fucking beautiful."

Robert Johnson offered to buy him a beer.

"All right," said Black Elvis. "Molson's."

"Molson's it is." He was gone a few minutes, then returned with a pitcher and two glasses. "I like a beer with flavor," he said. "Micro-brews and such."

"I like beer that's cold," said Black Elvis. "I like it even better if it's free."

"Hard to argue with that, my man." He filled the glasses. "I'm sorry to hear about your friend."

Black Elvis stared at him.

"Juanita?"

"That's right. Tragedy. They say she had a bad ticker. She *was* a little overweight, now." He thought again about her. She'd had a lot of facial hair, he remembered that. And she used to wear this chef's hat.

"This is a nice place," said Robert Johnson, looking around. The next group was setting up on stage. "Real homey."

"This is the best place for ribs and blues in Atlanta. Don't let no one tell you different." He peered at Robert Johnson's round, white face. "So, you from Memphis, huh?"

"That's right."

"Memphis, China?"

Robert Johnson laughed. "I'm Korean, not Chinese. Well, my parents are. I was born here. But I've always loved black music. I grew up around it, you know."

"What kind of guitar that is you play?"

"Martin. 1924 00-28 Herringbone. I wish I could tell you I found it in an attic or something, but it's not that good a story. I paid a whole lot for it. But it's got a nice sound, and it fits with the whole Robert Johnson act, you know?" He adjusted his tie. "I've learned that it's not enough to just be good at what you do, you have to have a marketing angle, too."

"Marketing, you say."

"I've got me a gig here already for next weekend."

Black Elvis was quiet for a moment. "You been to Graceland?"

He laughed. "Graceland! Well of course I've been to Graceland. Everyone in Memphis has been to Graceland."

"What's it like?"

"What's it like?" He gave a silver ring on his middle finger a half turn. "Tacky. In some ways, it feels like holy ground, but at the same time, you also feel like you're at an amusement park. The Jungle Room is pretty cool, I guess."

"Sun Studio?"

"They have tours, but I've never done one. If you're so interested, you ought to go."

"You think so?"

"Sure. Why not?"

"You got connections there? Like who could get me a gig?"

Robert Johnson considered this. Black Elvis realized that he'd done exactly what he'd wanted not to do, which was to put this person in a position where he had power over him. But he couldn't get it out of his head that there was something about this meeting that was more than chance. He had a feeling Robert Johnson was someone he was *supposed* to meet, if only he could determine why.

"I don't think so. I mean, if you're going to do an Elvis thing, you're probably better off just about any place but Memphis. Of course, that's just my opinion."

"I'll bet they don't have no black Elvises."

"Are you kidding? Black, Chinese, Irish, Jewish, you name it. You think fat white men in hairpieces have the market cornered on Elvis impersonation? I know a place where they have a dwarf who sings 'Battle Hymn of the Republic' every evening at ten while two strippers give each other a bath, right on stage."

For a moment, he imagined a big stage—an opera house—with hundreds of Elvises of all shapes and colors pushing and shoving each other to get to the front. The thought made him shiver. "Don't matter. I'm an original."

"No doubt. If you don't mind my asking, what made you decide to start doing this?" He looked at Black Elvis with admiration. "I love your hair, incidentally. I mean, if I looked like you, Jesus. I'd be working all the time. You just have that natural, blues-man look. You could be John Lee Hooker's cousin or something."

"I don't care much for blues music," said Black Elvis. He sniffed. "Never have."

"Really?"

"I like that rock and roll."

"Well, whatever makes you happy." Robert Johnson made a move to get up.

"No, wait," said Black Elvis, suddenly anxious. "Tell me something. Is that what you think? Have I gotten it wrong all this time? Should I be doing something else? You play good, you sing good, you know about marketing. Just tell me and I'll listen. I don't have that much time left."

Robert Johnson stood up and adjusted his fedora. He looked slightly embarrassed. "I gotta go talk to a young woman over there," he said. "She's been staring at me ever since I got here. I'm sure you understand." He picked up a napkin and held it out. "You got a little nosebleed going there."

Black Elvis took the napkin and held it tight against his nose.

When he got home, Juanita was waiting for him in the living room, wearing her chef's hat and a stained serving apron, her wide body taking up half the sofa.

"You late," she said. "Did you have a good time?"

"Good time?" he said. He thought about this. He didn't really go to the blues jam for a good time. He went because it gave him a purpose, a place to be, and because by now it just seemed that if he didn't go, all hell might break loose. The sun might not come up in the morning. "I sang you a song," he said.

"That right? What you sing? One of them Elvis songs?"

"'Amazing Grace.'"

"Well, that's nice. You've got blood on your shirt, you know."

"Mmmm hmmmm." He pulled up a chair and sat opposite her. He had not turned on any lights, and her figure was shadowy and evanescent, like a glimpse of a fish below the surface of a fast stream. "You supposed to be dead, now."

"Supposed to be."

"Bad ticker, huh?"

"Just stopped on me."

"Hurt?"

"Shit yes. For a second it felt like someone hit me in the chest with a sledgehammer. Now, tell me the truth, how come you singing songs for me? You know I don't care for you much at all. I'd have thought the feeling was mutual."

"Let me turn on a light."

"Don't do that. I like it better in the dark. Come on, now, what's with the song?"

Black Elvis closed his eyes for a moment. "There was a man there, a Chinese man. He took my spot."

"And so you go all churchy? You just nothing but a hypocrite. Just a big old faker."

"I don't believe in you," said Black Elvis. "And I'm turning on the light."

"I don't believe in you, either," said Juanita. "Go ahead."

He cut on the light and she was gone, as he'd suspected she would be. From the street below, he heard shouting and laughter. He went over to the window and pulled back the curtains just far enough to see.

The two boys he'd seen earlier were out in the middle of the street. One had a spray can of paint and was walking slowly back and forth, while the other, the bigger one, watched and occasionally shouted encouragement. At first, he couldn't tell what the image was, but then the lines began to come together and he realized that it was him the boy was painting, Black Elvis, spray-painted twenty feet high and glowing against the asphalt. He watched in amazement as the details took shape, his pompadour, the serious eyes, sideburns, pouting lips.

"Believe in me," he said. "Stupid woman."

KNOW YOUR
SAINTS

Back in May, about the time that Larry's fiancée, Gwen, was coming
clean to him about the professor she had been sleeping with—apparently there was no book group or yoga class—his aunt Julia's
boyfriend, Frank Packard, had run his Alfa Romeo right off the
side of the autostrada. Frank, whom Larry had never met, was now
in a coma. "I'm just sort of waiting to see," Julia told him over the
phone, her three-thousand-mile-distant voice as clear as if it were
next door. "But in the meantime, there's lots of room here. You're
totally invited." That night at Loch Raven Liquors, as Larry shelved
case after case of Italian wines, the names began to stir music inside
him. Abruzzi, Montepulciano, Veneto, Valpolicella. When he got
back to his apartment—empty now, of all of Gwen's soft things—he
got online and bought a ticket, charging it to his already overbur-
dened Citicard. Pot smoke and the sound of bad guitar strumming
drifted up from the apartment downstairs; in the street, a man was
shouting at his wife. "I tole you," he said. "I tole you."

Julia was an occasional actress, in her forties, his mother's young-
est sister, and the oddball of the family, particularly in her choice of
men. She had once brought a guy to Thanksgiving whose entire face
was covered in Maori tattoos, even the eyelids. She'd been married,
briefly, but no one had ever met the man, and she never spoke of it.
Frank Packard was a different kind of choice.

"He has Alzheimer's," she told Larry his first night at the apartment, which was on the fourth floor of a sixteenth-century palazzo,
with a view of the Boboli Gardens off the tiny back terrace. Frank,
who'd had a successful dental practice in Buffalo, New York, had
some years ago moved to Italy with the intention of writing mystery

novels. But he'd started to suspect that there was something going wrong with him. "It's not too bad, yet," Julia said. "He's, like, sixty, seventy percent. I guess. I mean, I didn't know him before, so I can't be sure. Our deal is that I take care of him, help him spend his money and enjoy himself and, you know, not get lost. Then, later, he leaves it all to me."

"You have this in writing?" asked Larry, who was still jet-lagged.

"I guess that would have been smart," she admitted.

He asked if she was working and found out that she was spending her days in front of the Uffizi spray-painted gold and posed as an Egyptian sarcophagus, although it was becoming increasingly clear that she'd have to go home soon. Also, Packard's ex-wife was in town. "Buzzard," she said. "Just circling, you know?"

Larry spent his first few days drinking way too much, staring cynically at tourists, and copping poses with cigarettes that he hoped would be noticed by attractive women, but weren't. He imagined Gwen locked in a summer-long coital embrace with her new lover, taking breaks only long enough for him to explain the finer points of Marxist philosophy. Larry needed something to occupy his time, some sort of a project—otherwise his head was going to blow up. The town was full of art history graduate students giving private tours.

"Performance art!" Julia cried delightedly when he ran the idea by her. "I can help you find customers. I meet people all the time. I'll look for the dumbest faces and the nicest shoes. People with money always have good shoes."

"Let's not call it art," he said. "Let's call it theft."

He doubted he'd be able to pull off the deception for long, if at all. Perhaps it would lead to a fistfight. Secretly, though, he hoped he might meet a girl, someone to take his mind off his broken heart.

To his surprise, he turned out to be a reasonably good guide. No one seemed to know that "Massachusetts State" was not a real school (he had in fact gone to Hopkins, studied English, and played bass, badly, in a retro-punk band, The Meretricious Popes). Even for the clients willing to pay for tours—he charged a hundred euros for five hours—visiting the museums and churches was still mostly a duty to be fulfilled, a required purgatory to pass through on the way to afternoon gelato. They were not suspicious. There was a Japanese family of four who nodded a great deal and had him take their photo in front of Pizza Ponte Vecchio, then took his; there were Carol and Cliff from Ohio who were mostly interested in counting angels ("Look, Cliff, look how many there are in that one!").

He told the Japanese family that the pictures underneath various altarpieces at the Accademia were called the *pudenda*, and even got them to repeat it. He explained to a woman from Van Nuys that the Medicis had been crypto-Jews. He told Carol and Cliff that since Saint Peter was always depicted holding a key, he was the patron saint of locksmiths (Cliff was a locksmith). Some of the information he gave out was accurate—he'd eavesdropped on a few real guides, studied a guide to Florence he picked up at a *tabacchi*, and had done his best to remember information from the Survey of Western Art class he'd taken sophomore year—but he also made a point of saying things that were simply outrageous (though the locksmith comment, to his surprise, had turned out to be true). He told the Frankenthaler family from Bayonne that Michelangelo had done a series of pornographic woodcuts at the request of the Pope, and that these were kept in a special vault at the Vatican, too valuable to be destroyed, too embarrassing to be acknowledged. Before 1500, he explained, all depictions of Jesus showed the holy genitalia—loincloths were painted over later, mostly by Titian.

They met in front of the information office at the train station, as arranged. Bob Seitz was gray haired, in his midfifties, of average height, with overly tanned skin and a nose that appeared to have been broken at some point—it took a distinct turn to the left. He wore the kind of "travel" clothes you find in SkyMall catalogs—khaki cargo pants, a white, short-sleeved shirt, and a vest with an absurd number of pockets in it. He was allergic to something, and behind his round glasses both his eyes were rimmed red.

It was a particularly hot Tuesday morning in July, and Larry's hangover was bad. He'd stayed out late drinking Scotch and listening to an Italian band called Hard Again do covers of Muddy Waters songs. Bob Seitz shook Larry's hand enthusiastically, his grip powerful, the backs of his hands, Larry noticed, practically cobwebbed with hair. "Pleased to meet you," he said, and he really did seem it. "I'm looking forward to this."

They walked together to Santa Maria Novella. "Masaccio basically scared the hell out of everyone with this painting," Larry said, when they were in front of the *Trinity*. "They thought it might be black magic. Look how the figure of Jesus comes out at you."

"Who are those people praying?"

"Rich people who paid for the painting. If you paid for a painting, you got to be in it. Even a crucifixion. Noblemen and clergy show up—in Renaissance outfits—at the Annunciation, the flight into Egypt, you name it."

"Like getting your photo taken in Washington with a cardboard cutout of the president?"

"Exactly. That skeleton at the bottom is a memento mori—a reminder about death."

"I spent two hours in that Uffizi yesterday," said Bob. "You know who I saw there? Jeff Goldblum. Honest. He was with some young blonde. Very cute. But she looked, I don't know, maybe sixteen. Tell me about Saint Francis. What's the deal with him? What did he do? He's like Dr. Dolittle, right? Talks to the animals?"

Francis was Larry's favorite. "Classic case of dementia. The guy had a fight with his father, who was a merchant, his father disowned him, so he went off to live in the woods, where he basically had a psychotic break, or found God—you choose. Came back covered with mud and preaching, which in those days was a reasonable career path. Pretty soon he had followers, and the next thing you know, he's on key chains and coffee mugs. One of his big miracles was that he saw demons flying over a city, then sent one of his monk buddies to chase them away. He didn't even go himself. Personally, I think the demons were swifts. They're all over the place at sunset around here, catching bugs, darting around."

Bob had wandered up to the altar area and was looking at the wooden crucifix that hung there.

"The cross is probably by Giotto," said Larry, who thought he hadn't said *Giotto* enough yet today. He liked the way it felt in his mouth, like chewing gum. People always nodded reverentially when he said *Giotto*. "Notice the bones at the bottom? The medieval understanding about the crucifixion was that it happened conveniently right over the spot where Adam's bones were buried. Jesus's blood trickles straight down to them and boom—Resurrection."

"That Jeff Goldblum, he's even taller than you think."

"Is that right?" said Larry.

"After here, I go to Venice," said Bob. "This was a trip my wife always wanted to take." He made his way to a bench along one wall of the nave and sat down suddenly.

"Are you okay?" Larry asked. Bob sniffed, took a handkerchief out of his pocket, and blew his nose loudly.

Larry figured the best thing to do was to keep going. "Here's how to know your saints. Peter holds keys—those are to heaven. John the Baptist is always shown in a hair shirt. Francis is usually on his knees looking surprised as he's getting zapped from above by holy rays."

"Holy rays?"

"Then there's Stephen, who looks a little like he's joined the Mickey Mouse Club, with these round ears over his head, which

are actually supp   1at's my guy—holds
the grill they barbecued him on. Agatha had her breasts cut off, and
you'll often see her holding them on a plate. Like little custards or
something."

Bob looked at him.

"Oh, it's a celebration of pain and suffering." Larry checked his
watch. "OK, there's the *museo* next door, which has some pretty good
frescoes, although they're weathered, and then we go to San Marco
and look at the Fra Angelicos."

Bob stood and put away his handkerchief. "One more question,"
he said. "On this whole Resurrection business." He paused, blinking,
then continued. "The guy died, then came back to life, as I understand it."

"That's the idea," said Larry.

"Then what?"

"What do you mean?"

"I mean, where is he? If he came back to life, shouldn't he be
here?"

"Well, he went up to heaven."

"Alive?"

"Right."

"So, heaven is full of dead people, souls and all, and one living
person?" Bob dug into a pocket of his vest and produced a small vial
of pills, shook one out, and swallowed it with water from a bottle
that emerged from a different pocket. "I'm not trying to be difficult.
Honestly. Is it easier to care about these things, these saints and Last
Judgments and whatnot, if you believe in them? Or do you just look
at the pictures like it's a Superman comic?"

Larry saw that an actual guide—a young Italian man he'd run
into before and who he was pretty sure was suspicious of him—had
come into the church along with a middle-aged American couple.
"Superman comic. The Roman Empire never went away, you know. It

just transformed into Christianity, then continued to eat everything in its path. The cult of Minerva becomes the cult of the Madonna. Instead of lots of different gods to pray to, you substitute saints. People couldn't read, so the authorities gave them pictures to look at instead. The world hasn't changed so much. Back home, the cult of *Seinfeld* gives way to the cult of *Friends*, but it's all still the empire of American big business putting up the shrines."

"What do you plan to do with this degree when you get it?"

"I don't know," Larry said, thoughtfully. "Teach, maybe."

Bob poked a finger behind his glasses and rubbed his eye. "I'm in insurance. Claims investigation. Or I was. I'm retired now."

"You know *Double Indemnity*? I love that movie."

"Barbara Stanwyck," said Bob, revealing some teeth. "My wife was named Barbara."

Larry started toward the door. "Do you find many cases of fraud, then?" The real guide, a guy a year or two older than him, with Italian clothes—a dark silk shirt, expensive-looking trousers—was pointing at the cross and saying something about Brunelleschi. Their eyes met briefly, and they nodded at one another.

"Oh, sure. People stage or cause auto accidents, for instance, then sue for bodily injury. In Brooklyn, we get a lot of that."

"What do you do to them?"

But Bob didn't answer. His gaze had drifted back to the crucifix. Larry found a Life Saver and popped it in his mouth.

At the Museo, Larry identified various Old Testament stories for Bob in the frescoes, making up ones he didn't know. He should have been having fun—Julia had negotiated a fee of 150 euros from Bob—but he wasn't. He just wanted this to end.

In the Capella Spagnola, Larry pointed out the dogs on the upper right wall. "*Dominican* is Latin for *Dogs of God*," he said. "*Domine canes*. These guys thought of themselves as the Pope's SWAT team.

Dominicans and Franciscans were the Crips and Bloods of their day. Some monks even engaged in bare-knuckle boxing in the Lord's name."

"I used to box," Bob said, quietly, staring at the kaleidoscope of figures and scenes sprawling across the ceilings and walls. "How I got this nose."

They walked along Via Nazionale to Via Guelfa to Via Cavour through the heat and smog and traffic, Larry keeping up a steady patter of nonsense about Guelphs and Ghibellines. By the time they got to the convent of San Marco, he was exhausted. He checked his watch. "Listen, the monks' cells are upstairs. Fra Angelicos, one in each room. He's the guy the liqueur is named after. Heavy drinker, actually. I'm going to hit the bathroom. How about I meet you up there?"

"All right," said Bob, mopping his red face with the back of his hand.

When he got out of the bathroom, Larry sat on a chair and rested. A group of nuns passed by in light blue robes, their dark skin suggesting that they might be from Latin America. Then he climbed the stairs to look for Bob. He stuck his head in one cell after another, pausing to admire the frescoes. His favorite was *The Mocking of Christ*, with a disembodied head blowing air at the blindfolded Jesus. He was standing looking at this one, feeling the slight breeze that wafted through the window, imagining himself as the subject of the mockery, when he heard a moan.

He hurried out into the hall and tried to decide from which direction the sound had come. The he heard it again. Three cells down, he found Bob, crumpled on the floor.

"Hey," Larry said, kneeling beside him. "Are you okay? Do you need a doctor?" Larry had no idea how you even got a doctor in Italy. He didn't speak Italian, other than the few phrases he'd picked up to use in restaurants and bars. Bob looked up at him, his eyes lit with a kind of distant terror, and held out his hands, palms up. The center of each was bloody.

It occurred to Larry, just for a second, that this might be some kind of elaborate prank, perhaps even one Julia had dreamed up. But there was nothing particularly funny about what was happening, and no one shouted "Surprise!" Bob attempted to speak, but seemed incapable, and instead just mumbled. His wounds were real, and they were still bleeding. There was some blood on the front of his shirt, and on his cargo pants, as well as on the floor.

"What happened?" Larry looked up at the fresco in this room, which was of the Coronation of the Virgin, with various arrayed saints watching. Front right was Saint Francis, his hands upheld, clearly showing his stigmata. He looked back at Bob, who had the appearance of a person waking from a dream. There was no immediate apparent source of his injury—nothing sharp on which he might have gouged himself. The man was simply semiconscious and bleeding from the hands.

Bob said something else unintelligible.

"What happened?" Larry repeated, slowly.

"I'm not sure," Bob said. He got unsteadily to his feet and examined his palms. "I've got a handkerchief in my vest. Would you get it out for me? I'm a mess." Larry patted his pockets, found it and removed it. Bob wrapped this around his right hand, then carefully withdrew his other, used handkerchief, and balled it up in his left. He stood for a good thirty seconds, feet apart, eyes half-closed, as if waiting for an ice cream headache to pass. "OK," he said. "I'm fine."

Larry looked down at the blood smear on the floor. "Did you cut yourself on something?"

"I guess," said Bob. "I don't remember. One minute I was looking at the painting, the next . . ." He stared down at his two hands, now both closed into loose fists. "Oh, boy."

"I can try to find you a doctor," said Larry. "I think that might be the thing to do. I mean, if you want. Would you like to go to a doctor?"

"I hate doctors, and I don't speak the language. I go to some Italian doctor, I'll end up having my tonsils out."

"Are your feet okay?"

"What do you mean? What would be wrong with my feet?"

"Never mind," said Larry. "I'm sure you're right. It's nothing."

Bob brought his hands up in front of his chest and peered cautiously inside, then let them fall again. "Maybe we should go now."

"Yes," said Larry. "Absolutely. Where would you like to go?"

"I don't know."

"How about your hotel?"

"Sure. Okay."

But when they were outside, it became clear that Bob was confused. He leaned up against the side of a building. "Could we go back to your place?" he asked.

"Not the hotel?"

"This is hard to admit, but I'm afraid to be alone."

"And you're sure you don't want a doctor?"

Bob unclasped one hand and examined the palm, holding it in such a way that Larry could not see. "You got bandages at your place? Maybe some iodine? That ought to take care of it."

"What the hell happened in there?" Larry asked.

"I'm telling you, honestly, I have no idea."

Julia was not home when they got to the apartment. Bob went into the bathroom and stayed a long time. When he came out, he had gauze around both hands. "They're still bleeding."

"Bleeding a lot?"

"Not a lot. Kind of oozing, you might say." He examined a photo of Gwen Larry had stuck onto the refrigerator door. It had been taken on top of Federal Hill, and it showed her framed by an impossibly blue sky, Baltimore's Inner Harbor spread out behind her. She looked very pretty in jeans and a white shirt, her hands on her hips, her eyes squinted against the sun. Larry had regular, rational conversations with her in his dreams ("Why did you do it? What were you thinking about while you were doing it?"), and in them she always looked exactly like she did in this picture, smiling, secret, her true self locked away.

"This is strange," said Larry. "I don't know what to tell you. Maybe you can go on one of those afternoon talk shows."

Bob turned away from the photo. "What I'd like most in the world right now is a drink." He smiled in a way that Larry had to admit looked beatific.

They walked to an *enoteca* just outside the city walls and ordered a liter of wine. Everyone around seemed young, beautiful, and coupled up. An American family at the next table grappled with their menu, sounding out the various choices. Syllables of different languages fluttered like moths in the early evening air. A cell phone rang and was answered with a sharp "Pronto." Motorbikes buzzed by, briefly filling the area with their acrid exhaust.

"Be honest with me," Larry said. "You did this to yourself, right? Like with a penknife or something?"

Bob's eyes widened. "A penknife?"

"Okay, okay. Do you have any history of this happening? Or anything like it? Sudden nosebleeds, for instance? What are those pills you take?"

"Heart medicine. They don't make your palms bleed." He took a long swallow from his wine. "I pinched your sister."

"You did what?"

"On the butt. I couldn't help myself. I get around women, I don't know what to say to them. I pinched her, and then she talked to me about hiring you for a tour, and I couldn't say no. Maybe it's punishment."

"Well, this sort of thing isn't usually about punishment."

"What, then? What's it about? You're the expert."

"A reward, I think. Sort of."

"Some reward." Bob's eyes flickered shut, then open. "She told me about her boyfriend. It took my wife three years to die. She tried everything—shark cartilage pills, coffee enemas, meditation. Over time, you start to pull away. You're impatient. Every night, I'd think about the life I was going to have after she was gone." He pulled aside one of his bandages with the forefinger of his other hand and peered underneath. "I had various plans. One was to move to Australia and live by the beach. Another was to get a degree in something. Law, maybe, or economics. I'd be the old guy in class everyone wondered about. I also thought I could take up the trumpet. You like Herb Alpert?"

"Who?"

"'The Lonely Bull'? It's beautiful—like a whole movie in a two-minute song. You feel the sadness of the bull. And then you hear the crowd, cheering. Cheering. It's really something."

"I don't know it." Larry eyed Bob's pockets. Perhaps one of them contained a knife, or a corkscrew, and Bob had dug away at his palms with it, then stuck it back in. Larry could think of no earthly reason for Bob to have done this.

"She wouldn't die," he said. "The prognosis was one year. When it gets to three, that's not dying anymore, that's living."

Larry took a sip of wine. "Did you know that Saint Lorenzo, as they were grilling him, made a joke to his torturers? He said, 'I think I'm done on that side—go ahead and turn me over.'"

"What should I do?" Bob asked. Larry thought there was something panicked in the man's eyes.

"You should keep them bandaged and don't tell anyone. Couple of days, they ought to heal up fine." He thought of psychosomatic illnesses—hysterical pregnancies, hysterical blindness. The human body was capable of all sorts of betrayals.

"She's got a nice butt, your sister."

"Excuse me?"

"Tight, like a honeydew." He grinned, showing teeth the color of weak tea.

"She's my aunt. And I don't need to hear that."

"She likes older men, it seems like."

"I don't know what she likes. I can't speak for her. You shouldn't be pinching statues anyway."

"Like a honeydew."

"You know what?" said Larry, waving for the waitress. "The tour is over."

Larry put Bob into a taxi and sent him back to the Hotel Vasari, then walked himself back to the apartment, where he settled into Frank Packard's overstuffed green chair and flicked on the television to an Italian game show he couldn't follow at all. He did his best to put Bob entirely out of his mind. The guy had problems. He'd probably dug at his own palms somehow. And if he hadn't? Well, maybe God did have a sense of humor. Feeling thirsty, he went to the refrigerator for one of Julia's Diet 7UPs. That was when he noticed the blank space on the door.

He tried to think of some moment when Bob could have stolen the photo of Gwen, but couldn't—it seemed a magic trick. He stood frozen, unsure what to do. Maybe Bob had done him a favor. Even Julia had commented on the dubious wisdom of keeping her up there. "You'll never get anyplace," she said, "if you insist on looking backwards at where you've been, and not forward at where you might end up." On the other hand, the photo was the only thing he had that he cared about at all. Without even bothering to shut off the TV, he headed out the door and down the stairs to the street.

The Arno glittered with reflected moonlight as he crossed the bridge and headed toward the train station and Bob's hotel, hurrying in the still heat. He found the building and asked for Bob Seitz, but was informed he'd checked out.

"Checked out? Are you sure?"

The woman behind the desk was sure.

Larry walked to the station and looked at the board. A late train for Venice, a local that stopped in Bologna, was departing in fifteen minutes. He went downstairs and through the underground passageways to track nine. It was very humid, and he was sweating from the chin and behind his ears. He climbed the stairs to the platform and looked around.

Fifty yards away, a figure separated from a group of figures. Larry shouted, then began to jog toward him, but the man hoisted a small bag and got onto the train. Larry climbed aboard, too, and made his way quickly down the aisle to the end of the car. He passed through to the next one just as the far door closed, and now he began to run. In the middle of the next car, there was Bob, putting his luggage up into the rack.

"I want that picture back."

"What picture?" said Bob.

"You know exactly what picture." He looked down at Bob's hands, and saw that he now had on gloves.

"Florentine leather," he said. "When I bought them two days ago I didn't realize they'd be coming in handy so soon."

"Where is it?"

"I have no idea what you're talking about." Behind his glasses, Bob's eyes were still red and wet. The train's whistle gave out a number of short blasts. "I'm going to Venice and try to forget this ever happened. And I'm not looking at any more paintings."

Larry grabbed the man's shoulder. "You did it to yourself. I don't know what you used, but it wasn't holy rays. Here." Larry dug in his pocket and pulled out a wad of bills. "Here's your money back. Give me my photo and we'll forget everything. None of this happened."

"This happened," said Bob, and held up his gloved hands.

Larry dropped the money onto the seat. He was suddenly full of doubt about everything. Had he really seen the wounds? Could that have been an illusion, too? "Take them off."

"No." The train's whistle blew loudly.

"Take them off."

Larry grabbed for a finger of a glove, but Bob pulled his hands away and crossed them over his chest defensively. "Giotto, my ass," he said. "You don't even know Jeff Goldblum."

The whistle blew again, and Larry, out of time, hurried to the door.

When he got back to the apartment, Julia was home, making herself tea.

"I went to the hospital today," she said. "And you're not going to believe it. Frank is up and about. He opened his eyes this morning and asked how the White Sox were doing. It's a miracle." Steam snorted from the kettle as Julia took it off the stove. "How was your day? How was old Bob? He seemed kind of weird. I hope he didn't turn out to be some secret art expert."

"Nope," said Larry, watching her carefully fill a mug. "He didn't know the first thing."

COWBOY
HONEYMOON

Kaufman drove from one fire to another. In Baltimore, there had been a train wreck in the Howard Street Tunnel, the northern end of which was not far from the small house he owned, tucked away on a side street behind the hulking wreck of a Victorian hotel, and three doors down from a gay bar with no sign or windows. The train was loaded with toxic chemicals, and stuck in the tunnel as it had been, there was little the authorities could do. The downtown air filled with the smell of melted plastic and electrical wire. Temperatures reached a thousand degrees in the tunnel, so hot that the cars glowed.

In Jackson it was wood smoke, thick as a campfire when the wind blew from the south. A whole mountainside was burning. Fat insect helicopters traveled back and forth from the airport, huge baskets dangling under them like egg sacs. Around town, signs everywhere read, "Thank you, firefighters!" The air hurt your eyes, and Kaufman had to run his wipers to clear ash from the windshield of his Subaru.

Everything in the hotel bar gleamed, from the hanging racks of stemware, to the long, polished mahogany bar itself, to the picture windows in the seating area. They were atop a mesa, with views in all directions. Kaufman felt as if he'd been somehow transported to the pages of the kind of magazine he'd never read on purpose.

"See that couple?" asked Rhonda. It was cocktail hour at The Blue Buffalo. After one day working for Irving Straight, Kaufman was already wondering about his decision. The man did huge, saccharine oils with titles like *Beddin' 'em Down* and *Chow Time*, depicting sunburnt Marlboro men, cows and horses at twilight.

At a table by the window, he observed a woman who looked to be in her midthirties, with frizzy dark hair and black plastic-framed glasses. The man with her seemed somewhat older, had a shaved head, and looked bored.

"Yes," he said. "I see them."

"They're here through an Internet auction—one of those travel sites. Only when she got here this morning and saw their room, she pitched a fit and said it was their honeymoon. They had room 11. It's small, and there isn't any view. She starts crying right there, I mean sobbing. What a show."

"You think she's lying?"

"Of course she's lying. She's some spoiled East Coast chick."

"What did you do?"

"I gave her the honeymoon suite." Rhonda applied Chap Stick to her lips. Her hair was tinted blonde, her skin tanned and creased around the eyes, and yesterday Kaufman had noticed a geometric tattoo barely rising out of the back of her jeans, the same as a lot of his students had back in the city.

"That was nice of you," he said.

"It was available. With the fire, I'm getting cancellations like crazy. But I want to have some fun with them. I really want to push this. There is no way they're married. I don't even think he wants to be here, to tell you the truth."

"How do you know? They're wearing rings."

"That doesn't mean anything—I wear a ring. You get to a certain age, you just do. Hell, he might be married to someone else. Anyway, they've got reservations for dinner here tonight, and I've arranged to have a cake appear. I'm having Paco decorate their table with balloons, and the wait staff are going to come out and sing. You should have seen her, crying like a six-year-old. Like the world owes her something. Know what I wish you'd do? Hit on her. It'll be good practice for you, and who knows? Maybe you'll get lucky."

Kaufman looked again at the woman, tried to imagine starting some kind of conversation. Jackie, the girlfriend he'd moved in with after college but never married, had died almost ten years ago, and though he'd dated on and off since then, it hadn't been with much success. There was no one in his life right now, although he liked to think he had prospects—the young blonde he'd met in his last painting class, for instance, who liked Elvis Costello. Or the antiques dealer he'd met recently at The Walters on Rhumba Night, who was interested in old maps (there had been an exhibit on). Who was he kidding? The blonde was twenty-three, maybe younger, while Kaufman was forty-two, surely out of her range. The antiques woman seemed to believe that Greek civilization had followed, and indeed improved upon, that of Rome. He had no prospects. "I don't hit on married women."

"Here's what I'm telling you. That woman is in an unhappy relationship. She might sleep with you just to push things with *him*."

"What would that say about me?"

"I'm sorry, Skip. You're right. You need another drink?" She was the one who'd given him the nickname, and he didn't even know why. That was being a younger brother—eight years old and one day you suddenly had a new name, which no amount of protest was going to change. Even his parents had begun using it.

"Please. I had a hard day on the range." As he said this, he noticed that the man was getting up.

"Go downtown and see what Irving's paintings are selling for. Forty thousand bucks. For that kind of money, maybe you could paint a few Indians."

"It's kitsch."

"Of course it's kitsch. What did you expect? People around here pay a couple of million dollars for a log cabin in the woods that has a Jacuzzi, hot tub, and Sub-Zero, they need something atmospheric for the walls. Irv also happens to be a very fine painter. In the world of Western art, he's very highly thought of."

The woman was now alone, and she did seem sad. "I don't doubt it," he said.

"Ooh." Rhonda poked his arm. "Go over and bring her another margarita. Compliments of the house. Talk to her."

"How?"

"Just ask her how she's enjoying herself."

"Maybe, but on one condition. You go do something else."

"All right. I have to make some calls anyway. But I want a full report."

Kaufman went to the bar, had Dreadlock Steve mix two margaritas, then brought them to the woman's table.

"On the house," he explained. "I wonder if I could join you. That is, if you're alone."

"I'm alone," she said, eyeing the drink he held out. She motioned with her head toward the opposite chair, and Kaufman slid into it. "My husband has gone to the room to play mandolin."

"A musician."

"I didn't say that." She had high cheekbones, wide-set green eyes. "Are you related to that manager?"

"You're good. Most people don't see the resemblance."

"Well, I see it."

"Can I tell you something?"

"What?"

He leaned forward, and was pleased that she did, too. Their faces were only inches apart. He very much wanted to touch her. "My sister doesn't believe you're married."

"Sure she does," she whispered. "She gave us the honeymoon suite."

"Because you cried."

"I cry all the time. It doesn't mean I'm lying."

Kaufman sat back, and so did the woman. He felt as if they'd known each other a long while, and he couldn't explain it. He'd heard of people having chemistry, but he'd never quite known what the expression meant. Perhaps this. "All the smoke in the air sure makes for a nice sunset."

"You like sunsets?"

"It's in my job description. I'm a painter. I'm working for a famous Western artist right now, finishing his stuff. I can't tell you his name. I had to sign a contract."

"Finishing what parts?"

"Scenery, bodies. He does faces, and he does the underpaintings, but I do a lot of the filling in. Right now, I'm working on a boulder."

"Is that ethical?"

"A boulder?"

"The whole thing."

"I think so."

She was looking out the window again. The shirt she had on was sleeveless, and her long, thin arms were nicely muscled. "Well, I guess it's not surgery," she said. "Anyway, I am."

"Sorry?"

"Married. And this is my cowboy honeymoon."

"My sister's probably jealous. She's older than I am, and neither of us is married."

"You ought to try it. It's everything it's cracked up to be and more."

"Look at that fire," he said.

"You don't think we're in hell, do you?" She took a long swallow from her drink.

He didn't think this was going all that well. "What do you do?"

"I'm in advertising. I dream up amusing scenarios for selling things. You know those milk ads where a cow comes walking through that family's living room while they're watching TV? That's one of mine."

Kaufman pretended to know what she was talking about, even though his TV had died two years ago during a thunderstorm, an electric bleat of protest before falling silent. He had yet to replace it. "Are you from New York?"

She nodded, drew a circle in the frost on the side of her glass with her finger. "Hey, you want to go for a hike tomorrow?"

"Sure. What about your husband?"

"His plantar fasciitis is acting up. I want to do Jenny Lake."

"I'm supposed to work in the morning, but I could go around one."

"Then we'll meet at the front desk," she said, cheerily. "It's a date."

Kaufman did not stick around for the cake. Instead, he got a burrito at a place in town, then walked briefly around the square, looking in the windows of the various galleries and souvenir shops. He felt exhilarated, strange. The salt from the margaritas had left him thirsty, the air didn't contain enough oxygen, and his heart seemed to be working overtime. He saw a kid lose three scoops of ice cream in what appeared to be slow motion, watched all the while by a fascinated collie tied to a parking meter a few yards away.

Irving Straight's studio was a separate building behind a modest house five blocks south of the town center. He'd shown Kaufman where he hid the spare key under a cinder block beside the house, and now Kaufman let himself in. He liked the clutter of a studio, the sense of work ongoing, the random splotches of color that accumulated on everything. A big oak desk with a combination TV and VCR on it took up much of one wall, and various videocassette tapes were piled up alongside. Straight believed in keeping old Westerns playing for atmosphere. Already, Kaufman had listened to *Red River* and *El Dorado*.

He went to the painting he'd been working on and took another look at his boulder. There was a rattle of movement behind him as Irving Straight came in. He was in his late fifties, with white hair he combed straight back, and oversized glasses that magnified his eyes out of proportion to the rest of his face. He wore a droopy handlebar moustache.

"A burglar," he said. "I hope you don't have a gun." He went to the boulder and stuck his face right up to the canvas, then backed away.

"What do you think?"

"Try a smaller brush. And try to think a little more cowboy. Think Gary Cooper, Randolph Scott, maybe even Lee Marvin. Henry Fonda, for that matter."

"Those are actors."

"I know they're actors, Art School. That's not the point. It's what they embody, the whole spirit of the thing. I don't know if this is going to work out."

Kaufman looked at his boulder. "I'll try harder," he said.

"I wasn't keen on hiring you, you know, considering the circumstances with Rhonda and me. I thought it might just muddle the waters. But she can push a point when she wants to. I used to fix cars for a living. You were a teacher, right?"

Kaufman thought how odd that use of the past tense sounded. He'd taught his last class less than a month ago. What was he now? Starting over. A colleague of his had dropped dead back in the spring, and he was only forty-five. Two weeks later, Kaufman had submitted his resignation. It didn't make him feel brave, or even particularly nervous. It felt like the only thing he *could* do.

"Circumstances?" he asked.

Irving Straight took a bottle of water out of the small refrigerator under the window, unscrewed the cap, and took a swallow. "She didn't tell you about us?"

"She just said you were friends."

"I've known her five years now, but only for the past two was it romantic. Up until last month, when I called it off."

Rhonda had dated a drug dealer in high school, and Kaufman could still hear the purr and hack of his idling motorcycle outside their house late at night as he'd drop her off. Her subsequent relationships had all seemed influenced by that unfortunate paradigm, and Kaufman didn't ask many questions. "I didn't go to art school," he said. "I just took a few classes."

"She wants to get married," said Straight. "I already did that, thirty years ago, and I wasn't good at it. Ask my ex-wife, ask my two kids. What I'm good at is right here in this room—I paint my pictures, and then I have a girlfriend for my not-painting time. It might sound hard, but it's the facts. I never represented it different, and Rhonda knew that all along. I hired you because I think you can do the work, not because I feel guilty. That's all. But you have to show me that you *can* do the work." He returned the water to the fridge. "That's not getting it," he said. "You want to go have a real drink?"

At The Cowboy Bar, the men wore ball-strangling Wranglers with big belt buckles, Western shirts, and moustaches; the women all had long hair, hip-hugger jeans, midriff-revealing tops, and serious makeup. Everyone had on a hat. Kaufman followed Irving Straight to a table, sat, and ordered the same thing he did—a double Jack Daniels on the rocks. He could tell the tourists from the locals fairly easily. In Baltimore, there was only one bar he went to regularly, right in his neighborhood, because he liked their grilled chicken sandwiches. Otherwise, he'd become a recluse, moving between his living room, the kitchen, the bedroom upstairs, and the spare room where he painted.

"Rhonda likes this place," said Irving Straight.

Kaufman looked at his watch and wondered if dinner was over back at the hotel. "How does it feel to get forty thousand dollars for a painting?"

"I wouldn't know. The gallery takes fifty percent. But, yeah, I see what you're driving at." He cracked a knuckle. "It's a kick in the ass." He sipped his drink. "So, look, just tell me one thing. She's seeing someone new, right?"

"I don't know," said Kaufman.

"You don't?" His eyes floated behind his lenses like pond creatures. Kaufman had the impression that Irving Straight was honestly surprised by moments when the world appeared not to be entirely about him.

"Okay, yeah, she is. A mandolin player." The band was playing an old Little Feat song that Kaufman recognized, and could remember Jackie singing along to back in their apartment on Guilford Avenue. The thrift shop furniture, the tattered stereo speakers up on cinder blocks. *Put on your sailing shoes.* He'd have called that rock, back in the seventies, but now he saw how it might have been country. On a talk radio show somewhere near Omaha, he'd heard a caller say, "I know hindsight is fifty-fifty, but . . ." He'd liked that, even repeated it aloud. As he'd driven, Kaufman had stored each brief passing image—an abandoned gas station, a collapsing barn, a gleaming new mall set like a child's toy amid the cornfields—in his mind. These things were unambiguous.

"Being an artist means sacrifice, man," said Straight, poking at an ice cube. "Don't fool yourself. Happiness doesn't have anything to do with it, and neither does getting laid."

Kaufman was awakened by his sister on the phone at a little after 7:00 a.m. His room was similar to the regular guest ones, except that it was located by the service building, which housed gardening equipment and large electric pumps that came on and off all night long. "So, where did you go last night?" she asked.

"Into town. I had drinks with Straight." Kaufman picked sleep out of his eyes and squinted at the bright light seeping through the blinds.

"Tell me about the margaritas," she said.

"You're probably right about the husband, if that's what he is. What happened with your cake?"

"She's such a phony. They fed each other pieces and everyone applauded."

"We're going for a hike this afternoon to Jenny Lake."

"You are? Now this is exciting. How'd you manage it?"

"It was her idea. I think he has something wrong with his feet, so he couldn't go. By the way, what's her name?"

"Are you serious?"

"It just never came up."

"Elizabeth Moore. Boring, huh? Hey, I need you to tend bar for a couple of hours tonight. Steve's band has a gig, so I gave him the night off."

He sat up further in the bed. "OK. I gotta get going here," he said. "I have a boulder to finish, and then later I get promoted to cattle."

Straight wasn't at the studio, but he'd left scrawled instructions on a couple of Post-it notes. The first read, "Do Cows." On the wall behind the easel there was a rough sketch of what the finished painting was supposed to look like. One cowpoke sat resting against a boulder, holding out a cigarette, while another leaned down toward him, his hands cupping a lighter. A bit to the right was a horse, and in the distance, moving up and toward the vanishing point, were lots of cows, represented at this point by lightly sketched shapes.

Do cows. On the canvas itself, Straight had already penciled in the closer cows, as well as their faces. The ones that receded into the distance were probably what he meant, but Kaufman, who was used to working from photographs, had an idea. He poked through the stacks of art books piled against the wall until he found what he wanted, a fifteenth-century Flemish nativity scene. The Christ child at the center, casting light outward onto the faces of Mary and some admiring angels, and just off center and far less well lit, a bovine face, almost thoughtful. Kaufman mixed some paint and set to work copying it onto the face of the second cow back.

At 1 p.m. he was by the front desk, waiting. The air was even smokier today than yesterday. Coverage of the fire was national—*Good Morning America* had reported that over 3,000 acres were ablaze, with no rain in the forecast. Elizabeth Moore came in with a small black backpack and Italian leather hiking shoes.

"Sorry I'm late," she said. "You ready?"

"Your car or mine?"

"You honestly don't want to see me drive."

She smelled like vanilla and nervous sweat. He was somewhat embarrassed about the state of his car, which was still full of the detritus from his cross-country journey—empty fast-food bags, mostly—but she made no comment. They drove up past the airport, toward the mountains that jutted into the sky like jagged blue teeth. She chewed Tic Tacs, shaking another one out of a container every few minutes.

"They sang to you, huh?" he said, after a while.

" 'We've Only Just Begun.' It was humiliating."

"I warned you."

"It's harassment. Can't two people just be left alone on their honeymoon?"

"You don't get something for nothing. You wanted a fancy room, you're paying for it. Lots of people would be happy with free cake."

"I bid on this and won. I guess I should have known the place would be on fire."

"Sort of spur of the moment for a honeymoon."

"Hey," she said. "I'm that kind of girl."

They arrived at the parking area and set out on the trail, which went first through forest, paralleled by a gurgling brook, then emerged into an area which was far more open. There were lots of shrubs and short trees, but very few of any size, although quite a number of dead ones poked up like broken phone poles as far as they could see, their silvery trunks the color of polished bone.

"This area burned in the early eighties," Elizabeth said. "I read about it in my book. That's part of what makes it such a beautiful hike. You can see all around you."

It took an hour to hike to the lake, and they made small talk as they went. She was originally from New Jersey. She'd once thought she'd like to be a dancer. She loved dogs, especially big ones. Her favorite movie star was Vincent Price, her favorite movie, *Theater of Blood*. They found a spot to sit. "I brought cheese and an apple," she said, poking in her bag. "And these." She held up two brown and beige items about six inches in length. It took Kaufman a moment to recognize them as shoe inserts. "Orthotics," she said. "I snuck them out of his shoes last night. He's out wandering the town right now looking for a present for his kid, and I'll bet his feet are killing him. Funny, huh?" She made a strange sound in the back of her throat and her eyes filled with tears. "This is what I'm reduced to. Stealing people's orthotics."

"Look," Kaufman said. He arranged her apple and the piece of cheese on top of the rock beside them.

"At work, I'm known as the funny one. I did tell you I cry a lot. What is that, a still life?"

"Ever paint one?"

"I'm not what you'd call artistic. I'm funny." She sniffed.

"Look at the apple." He moved over so that he was right beside her. The light was coming from a slight angle. "What colors do you see?"

"Red," she said.

"Anything else?"

"I don't know. Darker red? Some brown where there's that spot."

"Good. How about underneath, just above the rock?"

She sniffed again. "Purple, maybe."

"Something close to that. It's the reflection of the rock itself. I think it's more a blue gray. But you're right."

"Are you going someplace with this?"

He wasn't sure. He only knew that he needed to keep her attention. "Being able to recognize colors is the key. That shadow, that's going to mostly be cerulean blue. Our red on the apple is going to range quite a bit. I see at least five different shades there, not counting what's reflecting up from the rock. The colors are in the light, you know, not the object. They travel in waves. Opposite colors—yellow and violet, for instance—actually seem to tremble when they're next to each other, because our eyes can't adjust for both at the same time."

She picked up the apple and took a bite, then held it out to him. "They're actually called *orthoses*. That's what he calls them. *Orthoses*. It sounds like calling dibs on birth control pills."

Kaufman took a bite of the apple and chewed.

"See, I told you I was funny." She got up. "You want to head back?"

He didn't move. He shouldn't have started lecturing her about colors. People didn't care about colors. Most people didn't. It occurred to him that he might never have a normal interaction with the world again. All those days he'd come into his class waving the *New York Times*, saying, "Who can tell me one thing about Liberia?" or "West Bank! West Bank of what?" That person seemed someone he'd dreamed.

"Wait," she said, and turned around. "Come stand behind me. Close."

He did this, almost touching her. She reached back and took

his hands, bringing them up under her shirt, placing them on her breasts. "Just hold me," she said.

He looked out at the flat lake, its surface reflecting the blue sky, but darker. They stood that way for a minute, and he closed his eyes and it was Jackie's breasts that he touched, though she had never let him—not again, after her diagnosis. After a few months, she'd moved out to be with her family, down in Virginia, which was where she'd finished up, spending her last days designing gardens in a small sketchbook. He'd gone down, of course, taking sick days, vacation days. But he'd missed the very end—she'd just slipped away one night while he was putting together a lesson plan. Her mother asked for her photograph albums; her brother wanted her books. The house he'd bought the following year had a small garden, but he'd never done anything with it, just let it grow wilder and full of leaves.

They took a different route back to town, one that brought them close to the burning mountainside. Kaufman had almost forgotten the smoke after this afternoon in the relatively clean air at the lake, but now he found it irritating to his eyes. On the news, they heard that the fire was 20 percent contained, which didn't sound all that promising. From various points on the road, they could see it pluming thickly off the mountainside into the sky. He thought again of those train cars stuck in the tunnel, glowing white with heat.

When they got back to the hotel, her rental car, a green Dodge Neon, had been decorated with shaving cream, *Just Married* spelled out across the back window in thick, white letters.

"You could admit it," said Kaufman. "I'm sure she'd let you keep the room."

"Never," said Elizabeth Moore.

Irving Straight came by a few hours later, while Kaufman was tending bar, wearing a freshly pressed tan shirt and a bolo tie. "I was over to see a guy this afternoon, lives in the Indian Paintbrush subdivision.

He has to get out of there by tonight. They're spraying all the houses with slurry in case the fire moves any further down the valley."

"Friend of yours?" asked Kaufman. It was 8:00 p.m. Earlier he'd served two nice-looking older women who stared right through him like he was made of glass, but now it was just Straight at the bar. No sign at all of Elizabeth Moore or her not-husband. He had the TV on, sound off, tuned to a cooking show.

"Customer—owns three paintings. Shouldn't never have built up there in the first place," he said. "None of them. Just a matter of time. These people with money get *arrogant*."

Kaufman thought of the painting from Pompeii of a woman picking flowers. Of course, it wasn't a resident of the town, just a decoration on someone's wall, but he'd always thought of it that way, as if he were looking at one last pretty moment in a life before the sudden wave of lava swept down and stopped time.

Rhonda came in, wearing a black silk shirt, open at the collar, jeans with high heels, and some dangly, Native American–looking earrings. She touched Straight on the shoulder. "Ready?"

"I'll be there in a second."

Noticing the surprise on Kaufman's face, she smiled. "Have fun, Skip."

When she was gone, Straight looked at Kaufman and poked him in the chest with a meaty finger. "Sint Jans," he said. "*Nativity at Night*."

"I thought a classical reference might be fun," said Kaufman. "Hey, it rhymes with *Injuns*."

"It took me over an hour to make that cow back into one of *my* cows."

"Sorry," said Kaufman.

"Any references in my paintings are going to be to *Stagecoach* or *The Searchers*, not the Northern Renaissance." Straight downed the rest of his drink and smoothed his moustache. "Damn nice brush-work, though," he said.

"You think?"

But that was all the man was going to give him. "This isn't a joke," he said. "This is what I *do*."

Kaufman closed up at eleven, locking the register and hitting the lights. He made a brief, unsuccessful attempt at conversation with Shari, the Navajo girl who was working the front desk, then figured he'd go read in his room for a while before bed. Through the lobby doors, he saw Elizabeth Moore putting luggage into the trunk of her rental car.

"Number 5 check out?" he asked.

Shari flipped the page of the *People* magazine she was reading. "Not to my knowledge."

He pushed his way out into the cool night. "Howdy," said Elizabeth Moore when she saw him.

"It's late."

"Exactly. But not too late."

The air was full of tiny specks of white ash, suspended, almost weightless, nearly invisible. An owl made a noise like a distant train.

"What about what's-his-name?"

"I killed him," she said. "He's back in the room."

"Killed him how?"

"Brained him with a mandolin. I'll need to get going now so I can keep a couple steps ahead of the law."

"If they catch you, they'll hang you."

"I reckon." She shook his hand. "I want to thank you for the lesson in colors. All that time I thought they were just sitting there, and it turns out they were trembling."

Words were like bricks in his mouth; he might have been a sixth grader asking a girl to dance. "If you ever come to Baltimore," he said.

"Don't even say it. I'm not coming to Baltimore. I barely know where it is." She sniffed her shoulder. "All my clothes smell like smoke," she said. "I bet they will forever." She looked at him, smiled. "Next honeymoon, I'm going on a cruise."

After she left, Kaufman walked around the grounds. No lights were on in number 5. He sat on a carefully placed boulder at the edge of the path and imagined her driving to the airport—where else could she drive to?—perhaps sitting in the parking lot for a while, determined to make her point, whatever it was, staring up through the windshield at the same ashy sky that stretched over him now.

His colleague who died had taught biology. On April Fool's Day, his heart had simply given out. A faulty valve or whatever—there really wasn't much to say, no lesson to draw from it. He hadn't smoked, had drunk only moderately, played basketball once a week with some other faculty members. His wife had thought he was kidding around. Their children were in college—the whole next part of their lives was coming up. They'd been having a beer and peanuts together at a pub, and he'd suddenly put his head down on the table and started to snore. She thought he was making fun of the story she was telling. By the time she realized, it was already too late.

From within, Kaufman heard the muted, tinny sound of mandolin strings being tuned. One of them kept slipping; there was the gentle climb toward unison, a moment where all was right, then a quick falling away. Probably, something was wrong with the tuning pegs, and yet the guy kept patiently at it. Kaufman could see how that sort of thing could drive you nuts.

THIS IS
NOT A BAR

I went to this new hotel downtown to hear my guitar teacher play. My girlfriend, Lorna, came along, although she doesn't care much about jazz — she plays classical piano. From the lobby, we made a left and passed along red halls with chandeliers lighting them, heading toward the hotel restaurant until we heard music. It was just a trio, upright bass and drums and my teacher, whose name is Arthur. They were set up outside of the eating area, in an open space between the entrance to the restaurant and a nice-looking bar about fifteen feet away, lots of burnished dark wood and brass fittings, which was completely empty. We took seats at the bar and listened.

"They aren't very loud," said Lorna. "I'll bet those people eating dinner don't even know there is a band."

It was a new hotel, like I said, and it smelled that way. New carpet, new paint, new everything. It made me a little headachy. So we sat at this new bar and listened for a while, waiting for someone to take our orders. After a while, a man came. He had a moustache, a thin one, and the badge on his suit jacket read "Manager."

"I'm sorry," he told us, "but you can't sit here."

"Why?" I asked. "We came to hear the music."

"I understand," he said. "But this isn't a bar."

"It isn't?" I turned and looked again. There were cabinets filled with liquor bottles, whiskey, vodka, various flavored liqueurs. There was a cash register, with one of those computer screens. Sprouting up from the center of the long, impeccably polished bar were beer taps with the usual brand names on them.

"I know it looks like a bar," he said. "But it's not."

"We're sitting here," I said. "Everything seems good to go. All we need is for someone to bring us drinks."

"It's for show," he said. "There's another bar, a real one, in the Chesapeake Room, if you'd like to go sit there. It's just at the end of the hallway."

I looked at Lorna, who looked back at me. She'd put on lipstick for this, and a pretty flowered skirt. We didn't get out all that much. "But there's no band in the Chesapeake Room," I said to the man. "We came for the band."

"I'm sorry."

"Really?"

He nodded. I could see the situation wasn't something he was proud of. "Look," he said. "I'll tell you what. Seeing as how you're here specifically for the band, you can sit here."

"Can we get a drink?"

He thought for a moment. "Yes, of course. I'll have to bring it from the other bar. What would you like?"

"A beer," said Lorna. "Rocky Oyster Pale Ale."

"And I'll have a Beefeater martini," I said. "Olives."

He was gone a long time. We sat, listening to the music. I held Lorna's hand for a while. We could see into the restaurant, and it was just us paying attention. There were a lot of mirrors in there, to make the place look bigger, and some tasteful little holiday lights had been wrapped around the fluted columns.

"My mind keeps drifting," Lorna said. "I'm barely here." She took off her glasses and smoothed her eyebrows, then put them back on. "I think it's the improvisation."

Between songs, I went up and said hi to Arthur, who seemed pleased to see me. He had on a white shirt and a gray sweater-vest, and looked more like an elementary school teacher than a jazz cat. "You should turn up," I said. "We can barely hear you."

"We started louder," he explained. "The restaurant manager came and told us to turn down."

"Strange gig," I said.

"You know it, man."

Our drinks arrived, the manager carrying them on a tray from down the long hall, so I rejoined Lorna. "Thanks," I said, and he nodded, then disappeared. We clinked glasses and listened to the next song. They were good, these guys — as good as you'd hear anyplace. It was pretty much a secret that they were working so hard; over in the restaurant, you probably got the impression of piped-in Muzak, or something.

The martini was solid — very cold. I was munching on the second olive when a scraggly-looking kid in an army jacket came and sat on the next stool. He waved to Arthur, and Arthur acknowledged him with a big smile, without breaking rhythm or losing his place in what he was doing, which was playing three different things at once: bass line, little two-note chords popping on and off like Christmas lights, and an improvised melody line on top. The guy was some kind of genius, and his fingers were extralong, slender, pale, and tapered. I didn't recognize the song, but that was hardly the point.

The kid kept looking around. Finally, I leaned over to him and said, "It's not a bar."

"It's not?"

I shook my head. "Nope. I know, I know, it looks like one. But it's not. It's a fake bar."

"But you have drinks," he pointed out.

"I know," I said, raising mine, then taking a sip. "They made an exception."

"If it's not a bar," he said, "why did they hire a band to play in it?"

"Your guess is as good as mine." There was something about his face I liked. He had acne on his cheeks and forehead, and curly brown hair that looked like he never brushed or combed it, but just showered and let it dry however. He reminded me vaguely of me, just a long time ago. I'm forty-eight; he might have been twenty-three. "Are you one of Arthur's students?"

"Yeah," he said.

"Me, too."

The manager came back to check on us. "Anything else?" he asked.

"I could use another," I said. I looked at Lorna, and she nodded. "And my friend here would like to order, too."

The manager wasn't sure what to do with this one, I could see. "Did you — "

"I told him," I said. "He knows it's not a bar."

"It's just for show," said the manager. "We have other bars. I really don't know why they put this one here."

"He's here for the music, too," I said. "Maybe you could break the rules for him, also? I'll bet he just wants a beer."

"Jack Daniels, actually," said the kid.

"Ice?" asked the manager.

"Ice," he said.

"All right," said the manager, then headed off down the hallway again.

We sat there, just the three of us, listening. The drummer was using brushes, whisking so lightly around the top of his snare that the sound he produced wasn't much more than wind makes shaking leaves from a tree. I felt bad for him — all the drummers I'd ever known liked to make noise. It was why they got into the business in the first place.

"I'm Andy," said the kid to me.

"Cleve," I said.

"Nice," he said, as if I'd just hit a jump shot. "Cleveland?"

"My dad was a history buff. It's better than *Grover*."

"I guess." He adjusted his balance on the bar seat. They were reasonably comfortable, wooden swivel ones with padding, but they had no backs. "He liked *Sesame Street*, too, huh?"

"I doubt he'd ever heard of *Sesame Street*."

The manager reappeared, saving us from the rest of this conversation. He gave us all our drinks and promised to come back and check on us later.

"That's Lorna," I said.

He nodded toward her, and she responded with a little smile and wave.

"Arthur's amazing, huh?" I said. "You been his student long?"

"Couple years." He was paying close attention to the music. "Nice," he said, appreciating some of Arthur's tricky fingering. He took a sip of his drink. "Huh."

"What?"

"It's not a drink."

"What do you mean it's not a drink?"

"I don't know." He held his glass up to the light. It looked pretty much like it ought to look. Amber liquid, some rocks. Lorna had taken to doodling on a napkin, and I could tell she was getting near her limit already. "It's weird."

"You want another?"

He grinned suddenly. "Sorry. Just my sense of humor. Thought it would be funny if this not-bar were serving not-drinks, you know?"

"Do you think I could smoke?" Lorna asked.

"I doubt it," I said.

"You can smoke in bars," said Andy.

"I think we've established what's wrong with that argument," I said.

He tipped his head to one side and looked at me with great seriousness. "How do you feel about the minor seven flat-five?" he asked.

"I don't really know how to answer that."

"It's probably my favorite chord. It's just so *there*, like your pivot foot in basketball. Know how I think about it when I'm soloing?"

"How?"

"Like a red ladder, leaning against a wall I have to paint. But instead of starting with the first rung, I step onto it a few rungs up. If I'm in E minor, so it's an F-sharp minor seven flat-five, I forget about the F-sharp entirely and just think *A minor triad*."

"A minor is red to you?"

"Of course it is."

"Are you synesthetic?"

"I couldn't say."

"Why a wall?"

"I paint walls for a living."

"Excuse me," said Lorna. "I'm going to see about a restroom."

"Make sure it's a real restroom," I said.

"Pretty," he said, when she was gone. "Your wife?"

"Not yet. I'm kind of doing her taxes. That's what I do. She's a real musician, plays all over the place. Recitals, accompaniment gigs. She made fifty thousand dollars last year."

"Damn." I could see he was impressed. "How long have you been doing her taxes?"

"Going on two years now. It's an open-ended kind of thing."

"I get it. Endings are overrated anyway."

"Hey, maybe we could jam sometime," I suggested. "Since we're both students of Arthur's and all."

"I don't know," he said. "Maybe."

"You pretty good?"

"I'm all right."

"Me, too," I said. "I'm all right."

I dropped Lorna off at her house. I call her Lorna, because that's what she says, but on her tax forms, it says "Laura." I tried asking her about it one time, but she just corrected me. "Lorna," she said. "My name is Lorna."

"I could come in," I said, now. "It's not that late."

"Oh, I don't know," she said. "I have an early day. I'm giving lessons all morning, and I have to practice for Seattle. And then there's this guy who's going to call me about a gig in Liechtenstein."

"Liechtenstein?" I said.

"The country."

"It's hardly a country."

"You're right. Technically, it's a principality. Apparently, you can rent the whole thing out for functions, like a Sheraton."

"Wedding? Bar Mitzvah?"

"It's more of a corporate deal. But they want music. German, preferably. This is some German company that's renting out the country. I think they make razors."

"Principality."

"Exactly."

We kissed a little, but not the very best kind — we were both sort of phoning it in. I ran a finger along the outside of her bra and she licked my ear. She was thirty, just turned, a secret late-night consumer of frozen edamame and watcher of *Friends*. "I'll call you," she said, and then she went inside.

I wasn't sleepy, so I went to this actual bar, Dapper Dan's, which is only across the street and down a block. A locals kind of place. I wasn't there more than a few minutes before Andy came in. I'd never seen him there before, but then I thought maybe it was sort of how you learn a new word, and then suddenly you start hearing it everywhere.

"Jack on the rocks," I said to the bartender, when he came in. "I'm buying."

"That drink at the hotel was nine bucks," he said.

"You should have paid them with not-money."

"Where's Laura?"

"Lorna," I said. "She went home. She has a recital in Seattle next week, and she's practicing all the time. Brahms, I think."

"Longhair music." He seemed a lot more at home in Dan's. The bar was just a converted row house, very narrow and very deep. A lot of cops drank there, and the food was pretty good, burgers and such. They had a fire going in the fireplace, and the air was thick with the smoke.

"You're doing her taxes, you said?"

"That's correct."

"So, you're, like, an accountant?"

"No. Years ago, when I was about your age or so, I got a job doing people's income taxes at this storefront office in Bedford-Stuyvesant, in Brooklyn. After a while, I took those skills to another office in Manhattan, a much more upscale place. Before I know it, I'm getting three, four hundred bucks for a tax return. Then they send me to represent a client at an audit, because no one else is available. The IRS says, 'We can't talk to you.' But they send me back the next week for another client, and the next week for another. Then in the mail I get this letter with my Enrolled Agent number. All of a sudden, I'm official with them. I figured it was a sign."

"Wow," said Andy. "I'm planning on moving to Manhattan. Do the jazz thing."

"I guess that's the place. I played in Manhattan, of course, back in the day."

His eyes lit up, and I could tell I'd impressed him. "Where'd you play?"

"When I moved there," I said, "that movie *Urban Cowboy* had just come out."

He shook his head, wrapped his large hand around his glass and took a swallow. "Never heard of it."

"It was a big deal at the time. People all of a sudden started buying huge belt buckles and cowboy boots and went line dancing. Half the bars in New York installed mechanical bulls. So, me and my buddy started a country band."

"Country is cool," he said, but I could see he was just humoring me. "Chet Atkins."

We got a little drunker. I decided to confide in him. "I'm trying to get back to my roots," I said. "I'm not really a tax guy."

"I get it," he said. "You've been faking it all these years."

"Exactly my point. I don't even know that much about it. It's not like I ever studied or anything. I just fill out the forms and send them in."

"Does Laura know?"

"Lorna. Not really. Although she may suspect something. This sudden interest in music, for example. All I ever want to do is talk about 'Stella by Starlight.'"

He shook his head and grinned. "'Stella,'" he said. "That's some deep shit."

"You know it, man. It seems to me that I took a wrong turn somewhere back in my twenties. I can't say exactly how it happened, it just sort of did. One day I was like you, all hopped up on Wes and Joe Pass and Pat Martino, and then suddenly me and my buddy are playing these electronic bull bars and singing Patsy Cline." I tried to remember what had happened next, but it all seemed very mysterious somehow, as if aliens had erased my memories and sent me back to earth with the outside structure of a life, but none of the interior part, the part that mattered. "And now, here I am, staring at fifty."

"You think maybe it's too late?" he asked. He looked concerned. His acne was a serious problem, and I wondered if he took anything for it. It was going to be hard for him to get women looking like that.

"I don't know. I have three ex-wives. Can you believe that?"

"Damn," he said.

"What about you? What's your plan for taking Manhattan?"

"Gonna head up there, bring my ax, start hitting the sessions. That's it."

He seemed to believe in some mythical version of the city, where Sonny Rollins walked the Brooklyn Bridge at night practicing his saxophone, where you might drop down into some tiny club on Fifty-second Street and see Bird or Diz or Mingus. I didn't see the point in telling him it wasn't true. Perhaps, if enough people like him decided it was true, it would become true. What did I know?

"It's all gotten kind of fake up in New York, too, these days," I said.

He nodded. The smoke was really getting thick in Dan's, like maybe the chimney was blocked up. "'Not yet,' you said. You thinking of proposing?"

"To Lorna?" I was a little surprised I'd let that slip. Before I could answer, a bunch of alarms went off. People from the back of the bar started getting up and moving in our direction. "What's going on?" I asked the bartender, but she wasn't paying attention. A big guy with tattoos on his arms sitting next to me on my other side said, "Fire."

We headed out into the street. There were maybe forty of us — an entire bar full of customers, just no bar to be in. Sirens approached, engines appeared. We already had cops — they'd been in the back eating the shrimp basket. I could see Lorna's house across the street and one block south, a two-story brick row house with her landlady's bicycle parked out on the porch. There was a light on in the upstairs window, which was her apartment.

For ten years now, Lorna had been performing and taking in checks, but she'd never filed a form. Not one. I'd met her when she answered my ad on Craigslist and she came by my office — well, OK, it's not an office, exactly, it's just a house, but my block isn't zoned for a business — with a box full of letters from the IRS and the State, all neatly lined up in order by the date she'd received them, not one of them opened. She owed, with interest and penalties, something on the order of two hundred thousand dollars. I was working my way through the years, trying to rearrange her past for her, whittle away at the debt. In the meantime, we were having some pretty hot, if occasional, sex.

Andy was talking to a cop. "What would I have to do?" he said.

The cop was one of the ones who had been eating shrimp, and he'd brought his plate out with him. He stuck a French fry in his mouth, chewed and swallowed. "Depends," he said.

"You must have some kind of guidelines, right?"

"Sure."

"So, like, what? Hey, watch this." Andy put his hands on the ground and kicked his feet into the air, executing a fairly smooth handstand. He held the position, then collapsed his legs back to the ground and stood up. "What about that? Public nuisance. That count?"

"Hardly," said the cop. "You have to be a lot more threatening."

The alarms had stopped, and the general consensus from the people standing around in the cold was that there had been a grease fire in the kitchen. What we didn't know yet was whether we'd be going back in. A passing car gave us all a honk. I guess we looked like we might be demonstrating against something out there, all of us standing in a group.

"Like if I gave you a shove?" said Andy. It seemed to me he was drunker than I'd realized. Bigger, too.

"That might do it." The cop looked at me. He was big, too, probably about my age, although stouter. He had a kind of weary look to him, and I thought I knew how he felt. "You with this guy?"

"Sort of," I said. "Depends on what you mean."

"What would be your assessment of his mental state?"

"He's a jazz musician. He paints houses. He's moving to New York. I can't tell you a whole lot more." I didn't think the whole bit about the red ladder would interest the officer much.

"Well, tell him he's close to getting what he wants."

Andy then put me in a headlock. This was quite painful, as I have some stenosis in my cervical spine — c-5 and -6. My left arm went right to sleep. "Now, I'm in trouble, right?" he asked.

"You got it," said the cop. He put his plate down on the sidewalk and pulled something off his belt. It wasn't a gun, exactly—more like a ray gun.

"Go on," said Andy.

"Nah," said the cop. "I can't use this."

"Why not?" said Andy.

"You want to fill out the paperwork? Because I sure don't."

"Come on. No one will say anything."

"You don't know the half of it. Reports, questions. This guy here"—he pointed at me—"he puts in a call to the *Examiner*, next thing you know I'm on the front page."

Andy let go of me. "Sorry," he said. "I thought I could get Tasered."

I rubbed my arm and waited for the feeling to return to it. "You need to examine your priorities," I said.

"Sometimes I get a little out of control," he explained. "I spent my whole childhood on various medications."

They weren't going to let us back into Dan's. "You know what's just about five blocks from here?" I asked. "Come on. We'll go see the lights."

"I've heard about them, but I've never been."

"Well, you need to go. Better than getting zapped with fifty thousand volts any day."

"You don't know that," he said.

We hiked over. It was nearly midnight. There's this block nearby where every row house does up the Christmas decorations. Plastic candy canes eight feet tall, plastic manger scenes, whirligigs and all kinds of trains on outside tracks.

"Wow," said Andy. "It's like a dream I had once. Only better."

There was a baby Jesus made out of electrical wire nestled in a cradle made of rusty hubcaps. There were wooden snowmen and vinyl elves and camels. A tour bus pulled up behind us and people started to come out with their cameras. "What do you know about Liechtenstein?" I asked.

"I think it's, like, a big tax haven. I read that somewhere."

We walked a little further. At the end of the block the decorations ended, except for an inflatable Santa on the roof of a dry cleaner's across the street, so we turned around in front of the hardware store and started back. I wanted to tell him things. I was full of advice, but I wasn't sure where to begin, or what the point would be to opening my mouth in the first place. I could tell him what not to do, what not to say, how not to go wrong along the way, or at least how maybe not to. He'd listen, sure, but it would just be sounds. I'd just be some guy who told him a bunch of stuff one night. He had to find it all out for himself.

"Hey, isn't that Laura?" said Andy, pointing across the street.

It was. Or at least it was someone who looked a lot like her. She seemed to be with someone. He looked a little like me. "Keep walking," I said.

IOWA WINTER

The week Junior died, the temperature dropped to fourteen below and stayed there. The seats on my Honda felt like they were made of plywood, and the engine groaned before turning over, a low sound like some Japanese movie monster waking up after a thousand-year sleep. I had long underwear on under my suit, but I could still feel my legs numbing up. Four miles to the funeral parlor, and the heater never did kick in.

After it was over, we all went back to Louise's for food. There was a big ham her sister, June, had brought down from Madison, and the girls, Maddy and Chris, were there with their husbands and kids. Louise had made chicken and seven-layer salad and brownies, and there was plenty to drink, too. I went to work on some wine and also took responsibility for the music. I played Willie Nelson's *Stardust* album, because I remembered Junior had liked it, and because I did, too.

Louise got me alone about an hour into it and pointed out toward the porch, where a lone person stood all bundled up smoking a cigarette. "What am I supposed to do now?" she said.

"We all knew this was coming. It has to be a bit of a relief." I didn't quite know what she was driving at.

"Not about Junior — that is a relief." She pointed again. "I mean about him. About Clay."

I sipped some more wine. It was good stuff — better than I'd buy for myself. I get the Mediterranean red, which is cheap but drinkable. "A man who'll step outside for a cigarette in this weather has to really love to smoke," I said. "I might join him."

"I don't think he has any plans," she said. "Neither of them did. And now that Junior is gone, I'm afraid Clay's just going to stay."

All along, I'd done my best not to think too hard about Clay and Junior. They'd met at a support group — I knew that. Coffee, cookies, a musty room in the basement of some school. The spring before, with Junior's health deteriorating fast, he'd moved back into the house, and Clay had come along. They looked the same — skinny and getting skinnier, big, hollowed-out eyes. Going through the same hell, it was easier to have each other there. I don't believe they were being boyfriends together, exactly — they were both too weak. Mostly, they watched TV, drank sodas and smoked cigarettes, counted out each other's pills. It was a good thing that Clay was around, particularly those last months, since it took some of the burden off Louise. But now I could see the problem.

"Can't he go home to his people?"

"His people don't want him. They disowned him a long time ago."

"Maybe he should have thought about that when he decided to embrace an alternate lifestyle."

"I can't go through it all again. You don't know how bad it was. With your own son, that's one thing. A person can do it. But I'm really afraid. You know how you read about old people, and when their spouse dies, they just suddenly lose their own desire to live?" She looked at me. Our problems were different. I had drunk myself out of this marriage ten years ago, but it didn't mean we weren't in love.

"You think he's going to die now?"

"I don't think it, I know it. And I won't have it happen here. There's only so much a person can do."

"What do you want from me?" I said.

"Tell him he has to leave."

I looked out at the figure on the porch. It was cold enough to freeze birds right out of the air, and he was calmly finishing his cigarette. A person in the process of moving right beyond his body. "Me?"

"Please, Lenny?" she said.

The twins, Kayla and Kaylin, ran past us giggling, each of them clutching a ham sandwich. "Those girls sure can eat," I said. "Maddy might want to think about putting them on a diet."

I used to have a nice little house-painting business. After I sold that, I drove truck for R. C. Reynolds up in Cedar Rapids, mostly routes in the Midwest. Paper products. Then I started to get lower-back trouble, and at fifty I went on disability. I was already out of the house, set up in my own place out here by the river. It flooded the first year, bad, and you can still see the marks on the walls where the water came to. I drank beer at the time, and I remember how when I came back from a week on Louise's sofa to survey the damage, my empties were floating around in the middle of the living room like barrel-shaped aluminum fish. Insurance eventually took care of most of it, but I learned fast that life by myself wasn't necessarily going to be a big bachelor party.

My second day in the house, before the flood, Louise came by with a bunch of dinners in Tupperware, each labeled neatly across the top: "Lasagna," "Meatloaf," "Soup Beans," and "Chinese." I didn't know what she meant by that last one, and I never did open it to see what was inside. It's still there. When I want Chinese, I'll usually go into town and head to Ding's for the lunch special.

For a couple of days after the funeral, I thought about it. I didn't want to get involved, particularly, but I did want to be helpful. This Clay person and I had at least one thing in common, which was that we'd been disowned by the people that loved us because of our behavior. In my case it was drinking and causing scenes, in his it was having sex with men. We didn't have to do these things. I knew that Junior's getting sick was more or less inevitable. Before he ever turned up back in Iowa City from San Francisco, I figured there was something wrong. He was still healthy then, still shiny and optimistic, talking about how he was going to write children's books, signing up for classes at the university. But I understood why he was back, and Louise did, too. And when he started to lose weight and get sick, we didn't ever even say the word, but we all knew. He was taking almost forty pills a day by the end.

I went by to see Clay. It was a weekday, and Louise was at work up at the hospital. I had a drink first, of course — Early Times on the rocks. It was good, but it didn't prepare me for what it felt like to step outside. Even with the sun shining, the air was a smack in the face. The river was solid as concrete, and the outer branches of the trees made me think of cracks in a windshield. I wondered if weather like this made them shut down completely, or if underneath it all they were still growing.

Clay was watching television in the living room. "Hey," he said, when I came in.

"Hey yourself." I stood over him. His cigarettes were on the coffee table, along with a can of Pepsi and a partially completed crossword puzzle. He was in jeans and a short-sleeved shirt that was too big for him and that, it occurred to me, might have been one of my old ones. "You want to get out of here for a while? Go get one of them three-dollar coffees?"

He grinned, showing teeth as yellow as a horse's. He needed a shave, too. "All right," he said. "You buying?"

"I am."

We didn't talk in the car. I found a space right out front of The Coffee Company, fed the meter a couple of quarters, and we went in. He got a cappuccino, and I had a Siddhartha, which the sign translated as "breakfast blend."

"That's a novel by Hesse," Clay said.

"I know it." We headed away from the counter and back to an unoccupied sofa that looked like it had come straight from some old lady's attic without any vacuuming in between. He sat on that, and I settled onto a chair opposite. There was a little table in between us. "It's still a dumb name for a cup of coffee." Someone walked past us with a teapot on a tray. "You know what *chai* is?" I said. "It's the Hindi word for *tea*. You order *chai tea*, that's like asking for a *sandwich sandwich*."

We sipped our drinks. The place was relatively quiet — a couple of tables away a grad-student type was clicking away at his laptop. A middle-aged woman was reading a book. Light jazz drifted down from hidden speakers somewhere above us.

"I think I can guess what this is about," Clay said, finally.

"What?"

"Well, when Louise had that trouble with the dishwasher, she called you to come look at it. And you fixed it the next day."

"Yeah."

"And you fixed that step out front last fall."

"I can do a couple of things."

"You want me to go."

"It's not me that wants it, exactly."

"Right. I get it."

I was thinking how easy this was. He understood the situation. I took another sip of coffee and felt something nice and comfortable kick in, like it does after the first drink of the evening. "So then it's understood? What needs to happen?"

Clay leaned forward. I could see all the bones in his face. "Lenny," he said. "There is no place."

"Sure there is. Don't you have a friend you could stay with?"

His eyes held on to mine. "Junior was my friend. Junior was everything."

"I appreciate that. But Junior is gone. You knew this was going to happen — both of you did. Didn't you ever talk about it? Didn't you ever plan?"

"No," he said. "We didn't plan."

"Well, that wasn't that smart then, was it?"

"Maybe not."

"You can't expect my wife to take care of you."

"I won't bother anyone. She won't even notice I'm there."

"What are you going to do?"

"I don't know," he said. "It's something I've been thinking about. There was really just one thing I did up until last week, and that was take care of Junior. Without him, I'm kind of at a loss." He laughed nervously. He had a very deep voice, croaky from all the smoking he did.

"What about your folks?"

"They don't know where I am, and they never will."

"I'm sorry," I said. "It sounds like a tough situation. I'm just here to tell you that you need to find alternate accommodations. Let's say in a week, all right? Louise — my wife — this past year has been hard on her, as you can imagine."

"You think this hasn't been hard on me?" For a second, I saw something rise up in him, a tough-sonofabitch independence that turned on a yellow light in his dead eyes, then went away. I recognized it, and I respected it. He took another swallow of his drink, and some froth clung to the corner of his mouth.

"I tell you what," I said. "You can come camp with me, temporarily. The important thing is that we get you out of Louise's hair. It's not a permanent solution, but I can live with it for a while." After I'd said it, I was a little sorry. But it was out there, and I wasn't going to take it back.

"I don't think so." He stared down at the table.

"Where will you go, then?"

He didn't answer. His face looked all clammy.

"You OK?"

"Coffee is hard on my stomach."

"Then you shouldn't drink it."

"I like to drink it."

"I'm giving you an out here," I said. "Be careful, because I don't have to do it. But I know that you meant something to Junior, and that carries weight."

"All right," he said, so quietly, I could barely hear.

I dropped Clay back at Louise's and told him he could move in the next day. Then I went to the library and did some reading. After that I headed over to The Deadwood and drank a couple more glasses of Early Times and started chatting up Nicole, the bartender. She's got enormous patience when it comes to me. One time she even drove me home, and it's not remotely on her way. I was so drunk, apparently, I started reciting Shakespeare, and I don't know any. She put me to bed and everything.

"Cold enough for you?" I said.

"Come on, Lenny," she said. "I don't get paid enough to listen to 'cold enough for you.'"

"You ever know anyone with AIDS?"

"Yeah." She lit up a cigarette and offered me one, which I took. She's got pretty hair. Graduated a few years ago with a degree in art, still trying to figure out what to do with it. "Why?"

"I'm taking in a roommate. Friend of my son's."

"I'm so sorry. I heard about him."

"It's OK. Life wasn't treating him so good. Now we got this other guy on our hands, see. You think it might be dangerous?"

"Not if you practice safe sex."

"That's not even funny. I mean silverware and stuff. Dishes. Just breathing the same air. Stuff hangs. I saw this program once where they showed what a sneeze does. Droplets in the air. You ever heard of HAART?"

"*Heart* like valentines? Like the kind that are always getting broken?"

"It stands for *highly active antiretroviral therapy.*"

"I know some of those words."

"Otherwise known as the cocktail approach."

"You mean pills."

I nodded and pointed to my glass, which was empty. I could feel a pretty good glow getting started, too, and I had an idea. The Early Times bottle behind the bar was about half full. I decided I would spend the afternoon killing it off and that would be it — after that I was through with drinking. I'd always known that someday I'd quit, and today seemed as good as any other. "I know a little something about the cocktail approach myself," I said.

Nicole smiled prettily. She had on big hoop earrings and a black turtleneck that showed off those small, high breasts of hers. "What do you know about it?"

"I know that it only works for so long."

I spent the whole afternoon at The Deadwood. Around dinner time, I drunk-drove over to the house, passing by the time-and-temperature sign outside the First National Bank, which announced −15 in numbers lit yellow against the dark sky. As I parked, I was conscious of all the normal lives around me in those 1920s-era houses, and I leaned on my horn just to wake them up a little. Ours was on Bank Street, a nice screened porch out front that I'd done quite a bit of work on over the years - - jacked it up where it sagged, painted it, put in new steps. Louise's car was in the drive — we drive the same model, though hers is a few years newer — so I knew she was home. I also knew she wouldn't want to see me like this, but that never stopped me before.

She was in the kitchen, but she came out to the living room when she heard me come in. She'd changed out of her work clothes into jeans and a fleece jacket and she had a knife in her hand. "Was that you honking?" she asked.

"Hell no. Louis Armstrong is out there. He's thinking to himself, 'What a wonderful world.'"

"You are sauced. Go on home. And try not to kill anyone on the way."

"I'm celebrating."

"What?" She gave me a puzzled look. "What are you celebrating? Did the price of whiskey go down?" She moved past me and gave the door a shove, since I hadn't closed it all the way. "I don't even want to think about the next heating bill."

"Where is he?" I said.

"Upstairs, resting."

"I quit drinking this afternoon."

"Go look in the bathroom mirror, then come back and say that again."

I needed to go anyway, so I plowed through the kitchen and into the little powder room we have off it. The temperature in there was a good twenty degrees colder than the rest of the house, but the plumbing wasn't froze up yet, and the toilet flushed just fine. The man in the mirror looked pretty good for his age. Still had all his hair, only some of it gray. Could have used a shave and a haircut. I picked a fleck of something out from between my upper teeth and tried to remember the last thing I'd had to eat. It looked vegetable, but I didn't think I'd had any.

When I came back out, she was chopping mushrooms.

"What's for dinner?"

"You can take home the rest of that ham Maddy brought. It's in the fridge. And the seven-layer salad — there's plenty, and it needs to be eaten soon. Did you do anything at all about what I asked?"

"Asked?"

"Oh, Lenny."

I picked a mushroom off the table and popped it whole into my mouth. "Of course. He'll be out of here tomorrow."

"He will? Where is he going?"

"Never mind about that. We've discussed it. I got him out of your hair. Call me for the tough jobs." The mushroom was dry in my mouth, and I stuck my head under the faucet to get some water to wash it down with.

She put down the knife. I saw that she was crying, just a little. "Thank you," she said, in a tiny voice that just about broke me down, too. "You don't know."

"At least things will be easier for you around here."

"It's like some strange shadow he left behind. With the wasting, they even look the same."

"It's OK," I said, "I've got everything under control." I reached out for another mushroom and knocked the entire cutting board to the floor.

I slept until noon the next day. Then I called to see if Clay was ready, and he was, so I drove over to pick him up. He was dressed in jeans he had to keep hitching up, and a dark green University of Iowa sweatshirt. He had two duffel bags full of clothes and an oversized leather briefcase. "Going to the office?" I asked.

"Meds," he said.

I stopped at Hy-Vee first so we could get some food, as I didn't have anything around the house. "What do you like?" I said. "How about we cook up some chili? Put some meat on those bones of yours."

We bought hamburger, chili mix, beans, canned tomatoes, Minute Rice, a twelve-pack of Pepsi, Pop-Tarts, chocolate chip cookies, Steak-umms, some frozen burritos, and a dozen bananas, among other things. When we passed by the beer aisle, I first looked the other way, then picked out a six of O'Doul's. My head felt like donkeys had trampled it during the night, but the feeling wasn't an unfamiliar one, and in a way, I sort of savored it, since I didn't figure to ever feel that way again. As we were headed for the checkout line, it seemed to me Clay was getting antsy.

"They got a bathroom in this place?" he whispered.

"Probably. You gotta go?"

"Uh-huh. Bad."

"Can't it wait?"

"I don't think so."

I flagged down a kid who was on his way to shelve some bread. He pointed back toward frozen foods, and Clay hurried off. I paid for the groceries and stood by the entrance reading the little notices posted there on the bulletin board. Tractor for sale. AKC-registered collie pups. A trailer for rent in Tipton. Hockey skates, barely used, $20. I thought about how Junior and I used to skate together sometimes, and then I tried to remember where our skates might be, or if they'd gotten thrown away somewhere along the line. Finally, Clay showed up. His face didn't have much color to begin with, but now, under those store lights, he looked positively bleached.

"You all right?" I asked.

"I don't really want to talk about it."

"Jesus Christ," I said. "All right, let's go."

Clay cleaned himself up and we had dinner, which I thought came out pretty good. We ate the way I always ate, in front of the television. Afterwards, I dug around the basement and found the skates. I brought them up and asked him what size his feet were. He was in the middle of taking two blue pills. That briefcase of his was divided up into sections, color coded. Some of the pills had to be taken before meals, some with them, and some after. Others were for first thing in the morning or last thing before bed.

"Ten," he said.

"Bingo." I held out the box. "Try these on."

Something like a smile flickered over his face and went away. In general, for expressions, he reminded me of those scrambled cable channels I sometimes found myself watching late at night — most of the time there was nothing there, but every now and then, like magic, the picture would come in clear as day. "Junior told me he used to play hockey. I got weak ankles."

"What's the difference?" I said. "I got a bad back. We could still lace 'em up and give it a shot for fifteen minutes or so. That river out there, it's like glass."

"You're nuts," he said. "Look at me."

"Come on. Believe in yourself." I held out the box, and he took it.

Just the effort of lacing them up wore him out — I could see it. He was breathing hard and sweating, and leaning forward he farted, which I made a point of laughing at to make him feel OK. I was sorry. Those ankles were like something you see on the History Channel, like something the Nazis did. His feet might have been tens, but they still swam in the skates, and it just made me think of Junior, and how I'd used to take him up to the field house Sundays to play with the rec league, what a solid young man he'd been. I started thinking hard about whether I had anything to drink in the house.

"I'm not much of an athlete," said Clay, attempting to stand. "I play a pretty good game of backgammon, though, if you've got it." He teetered for a moment, then fell back onto the sofa. "We going?"

"It's too cold," I said. "I don't know what I was thinking. But maybe if this breaks over the next day or two, and you're still here, we could."

I set him up in the guest bedroom, and he was asleep by ten. I could hear him snoring back there, surrounded by boxes full of my junk, old magazines and fishing tackle, a TV I'd been trying to repair on and off for years, a dusty 1985 IBM-clone computer (no hard drive) and amber monitor that never did work right in the first place, but that I'd hung onto because I-don't-know-why. I wondered what the hell I'd gotten myself into. I was feeling irritable, so I brushed my teeth, and when I was done I swished Listerine around in my mouth, but instead of spitting, I swallowed. That tasted truly awful, but it also gave me a sudden view of myself as no better than those kids you read about huffing paint, so I made myself a pot of coffee and drank half of it while watching a lunatic Australian on television prance around the desert picking up snakes. And all the while, I could feel the cold outside pushing in at the walls. Nature is hostile, no matter how hard we try to convince ourselves the opposite.

The next day I was sick. I hadn't gone twenty-four hours without a drink in years, and my body was in rebellion. Or maybe it was the flu. My stomach was loose, and I was running a low fever. Clay planted himself in my living room and did pretty much what he'd been doing back at the house, which was watch daytime TV and smoke, only here he didn't have to go outside. He did a fair amount of coughing, too. For a while, I came out and joined him, and we sat and stared at the shows together — he liked the crime ones, when they were on, but he also didn't mind the talk ones — but then I started to feel shaky again and I went back to bed. About an hour later I woke up and he was sitting on the edge of my bed, staring down at me.

"What's your problem?" I said.

"I was just wondering if there's anything I could do for you."

"Do? I don't know. Can you mix a good martini?"

He laughed. "Probably. It's been a while. Junior used to tell me about a place he went to in San Francisco — The Zam Zam Room. Some strange old codger bartended, and he made the best martinis on the planet, but you had to be really careful. Like, if you looked at him the wrong way, he'd throw you out. So you put your money on the bar and just waited to be spoken to. After he made you your drink, he'd tell you where you were allowed to sit. If you just went to a table and sat without him telling you, that was it — you wouldn't get served."

"You weren't out in San Francisco?" I asked.

"Me? No. I grew up in Moline. I never been west of Sioux City. Been to New York a couple of times. I liked that." I saw that face of his flicker again, this time with memories I was pretty sure I wanted no part of.

"OK, listen," I said. "It's nice of you to ask, but don't come in here again without knocking, all right?"

He stood. "That was a joke then, about the martini?"

There were ants crawling around inside my eyeballs; I felt all jittery. "I'm reforming my life," I told him. "This here what I'm going through, it's the necessary pain."

For dinner, we had leftover chili. I washed mine down with two cans of O'Doul's, and Clay had his usual Pepsi. We weren't talking, we were just eating. Then right in the middle of taking a bite, he put his fork back into his bowl and started to cry. I wasn't sure where to look. I had another bite, but what appetite I'd managed to convince myself I had was gone. There were visible cobwebs in a corner of the ceiling, and I reminded myself to remember them next time I vacuumed.

"Sorry," he said, when he'd more or less pulled himself back together.

"Yeah, well. Sometimes it can all get to be a lot."

"I wish I could skate." He was on the verge of losing it again. "I wish a ton of things. I never even got to be in a real love affair. Me and Junior, it was just a couple of young guys in old men's bodies."

"Hey, hey. This is his father you're talking to. I don't need to hear that."

He sniffed, blew his nose into one of the paper towels we were using as napkins. "Why don't you live at the house with Louise?"

"She asked me to leave. I wasn't very reliable. Used to disappear sometimes for a couple of days at a time. I might have hit her once or twice. But people can change. You know what you need? A project."

"I know it."

"I'm serious. You can't sit around watching TV all the time — you'll turn into a blob. What can you do?"

"Nothing," he said. "Last six months, it was all about Junior. Giving him sponge baths, cleaning up his messes, helping him in and out of bed, just everything."

I'd been in denial about this. When I had stopped over, which wasn't often, they usually had him already out on the sofa, cleaned up and ready to receive visitors. I hadn't wanted to know what went on behind the scenes. "You think that's where you're headed?"

He stirred his chili and didn't answer.

Then I got another idea. I was full of them these days. "What about that book he was working on? Do you know anything about that? Maybe you could finish it up. I know this girl in town, she's an artist. I could put you two together. She's a very good friend. What was it called?"

"*A City Dog*. Louise has it."

"That's great. Kids love dog stories. My grandkids do — all of them. Nothing better than a dog story. What do you say?"

"You don't understand. I have no talent. Junior was a good writer. He was musical, too. Some people just aren't born with that."

This was news to me. I tried to think of one musical thing I could remember Junior doing. I tried to think of one thing I could remember him writing. I could vaguely remember some finger paintings on the refrigerator door, but I suspected these were Kayla and Kaylin's, and it worried me that last week and thirty years ago weren't more clearly separated in my mind.

"Well, you think about it. I'll write down this girl's number for you, and maybe you'll give her a call. Might be a nice tribute to Junior, and maybe you could sell it and make a little money. I'm guessing you don't have any, right?"

I could see sweat coming out on his face, and I was conscious of it on my own, too. "I got some in the bank. Not much. I get disability."

"Me, too," I said. "God bless the government. Will you think about it?"

"Yes, sir," he said.

"That's all I want to hear."

He went to bed early again, and again I stayed up. This time I watched *The African Queen*, but seeing Bogart toss back whole mugs of gin made me change over to a biography of Rock Hudson, which was only slightly less depressing. Louise used to tell me I looked like him, back when we were dating, after I got out of the army, and it made me feel funny now, thinking back, because who would have ever pegged him for gay? And yet there it was, right on the TV, about how he was going out to sex places and bath houses, and all the while pretending that he was married to that sexy Susan St. James. Louise hadn't known the first thing about Rock Hudson, and I hadn't known the first thing about my own son, and I wondered if anyone really knew anything about anything, or if we were all just making it up, blind people walking through the world with our arms outstretched, guessing.

I slept hard, but not well. I dreamed burglars were coming—I even heard them open the sliding glass door to the living room. They took everything—the TV, my computer, the furniture, my great-grandpa's revolver from when he was security on the Union Pacific Railroad. They took all the silverware, even though it was just stuff I'd picked up at Target. They took all the framed family photos Louise had given me over the years. I knew they were doing this, but I stayed put in my bed, huddled, pretending to be asleep, not coming out until I was sure they'd left. When I did, I found they hadn't closed the door. Snow — it was snowing in my dream — drifted in and filled half the living room, sparkling and fine like sifted sugar, and I had to shovel it out.

I awoke conscious that it really *was* cold in the house, and I pulled on some sweats and slippers. In the living room, the door was open, although just a crack, and there was no snow. I pushed it shut, shivering, went to the thermostat and cranked up the heat. Only then did it occur to me how quiet everything was. Just the sound of the furnace cranking on and warmed air breathing up out of the vents.

I didn't need to check his room. I put on jeans and boots and a parka and hat and gloves, got a flashlight, and walked down to the water's edge. There's a little worn path that leads there, and at the end of it I nearly stumbled over a pair of high-top sneakers. Playing the light out onto the ice, I saw a shape about forty yards upriver, where Clay appeared to be lying flat on his back.

I tested the ice with one foot before stepping onto it, even though it was frozen hard enough to support an eighteen-wheeler. Then I walked out to him. He'd put on the skates again, apparently outside, which seemed miraculous, given how cold it was. Yet somehow he'd gotten them laced and tied. He was bare chested — his shirt and undershirt lay on the ice a few feet away, and his rib cage stood out prominently, descending fast to an almost nonexistent stomach that ended where his too-large khakis began. I learned later that one of the final sensations a person freezing to death feels is intense heat. It's so uncomfortable that you are likely to tear off all your clothes to try and get cool — this is one of the reasons that homeless people found dead of exposure are often assumed to also have been victims of sex crimes. But even without that knowledge, it didn't seem so odd to see Clay that way, arms and legs extended, almost like a person making a snow angel. His eyes were closed as if he were asleep, and an unlit cigarette jutted up casually from between his lips. The ice nearby was all marked up from where he'd wobbled around on those things, those skates of my son's.

I went inside to call Louise, late as it was.

IMAGINARY TUCSON

Joe can see it all in his head. At the president's reception in Byron, New York, there is caviar in silver dishes, expensive wine served by waiters in black tie. In a corner of the room, by an enormous window that overlooks the postcard-perfect, sloping front lawn of the college, its bright green tongue leading the eye to a horizon of gold-and-red-stained trees, Kate entertains three or four handsome young professors. She is tall, blonde, Nordic-looking, and her figure is shown off nicely by a simple black dress with a low neckline, but there is something else about her that has made her the center of all this attention. A sensuality, a promise of trouble and fun in her green eyes. She clearly knows about sex. Not in the way that other women in academia seem to know about it, as something they enjoy but also feel responsible for analyzing and deconstructing according to whatever approaches to meaning they considered in their dissertations. With Kate, there would be no apologies, just uninhibited pleasure. There is a man, of course — she's made that clear — but there's always a man. From their positions on the walls, past presidents and trustees gaze out enviously from their portraits, flat now as treasury notes. Voices rise and fall with clever remarks; fat shrimp glisten pink on snowy beds of crushed ice.

When Kate thinks of Tucson, she sees the swimming pool outside of the apartment complex where Joe is subletting, the weather blindingly sunny, with undergrad girls walking around in microbikinis. Long waisted, dark skinned, smelling of coconut oil and taco sauce, they have come over after class to measure out the rest of the afternoon one margarita at a time. Reclining in a plastic chaise longue is Kate's boyfriend, an expert on Denis Johnson and Cormac McCarthy and Leonard Gardner, muscly, tough-guy writers, out of one of whose books he might himself have easily tumbled. They love his Brooklyn accent, his sleepy, deep-set eyes, the slightly off-kilter look of his nose so that no matter which way you are looking at him, you still want to adjust your view. In between his East Coast origins and here lies some murkiness the girls don't really care about. Graduate school in the Midwest, a girlfriend who is also a visiting professor someplace. Someplace else. And now, Joe is going to play his guitar for them, as he often does out there by the pool, tanned and shirtless. He is so much more interesting than boys their own ages. He knows things - - about music and books and history and culture — and speaks of them with authority, always in that nasal accent. He's going to play a surfer tune — have any of them ever heard of The Ventures? — and they will get up one by one in their tiny excuses for swimsuits and begin to dance, their thin bodies casting rhythmic shadows over the blue pool.

Joe's tiny apartment, sublet from a French professor who is on leave this year, is full of pictures of other, nicer places: Hawaii, where she has a condo, St. Tropez, Nice. The across-the-hall neighbors run a nonstop party, and clanking, muffler-deprived cars pull up in the parking lot outside at all hours of the day and night, spilling out young Mexican men with cases of Budweiser. Between 10:00 a.m. and 6:00 p.m., it is too hot to be outside, period. He has tried to use the pool, but it felt like swimming in warm spit. The desert landscape here in the north of the city has been overlain by apartment complexes and the huge cement buildings of chain stores.

In between the lonely roads that connect these pockets of commerce, saguaro and cholla and agave and palo verde cook bravely. Sometimes, driving down to school, ignoring the smell of the waste treatment plant, he feels he's living inside a particularly spare Dr. Seuss illustration.

Kate's students wear dirty college-logo caps, and stare at her in class silently, defiantly. They have not done their homework — they have never done their homework. They deserve As because that's what their parents are paying for, and sure, if this were Dartmouth, they'd be working, but it isn't, it's the eighteenth-rated small liberal arts college in the country, respectable, but a perennial second choice and safety school. What does she want? They are, most of them, taking Latin because there is a newly instituted language requirement, and with Latin, you don't have to learn to speak. That's who she's got, the ones who don't want to speak.

The sky here (Leatherstocking country!) is the color of dishwater and has been for over a week. There is nothing to do. Nothing. The liquor store in the village boasts a complete selection of flavored schnapps, including "Oreo 'n' Cream," as well as a long row of Bully Hill Wines. The grocery store carries only iceberg lettuce, tight, cold balls of it, shrink-wrapped and shining. In bed at night, the sole inhabitant of the huge house they rented sight unseen, her nose is constantly cold. Winds from the valley sweep up the hill and batter and shake the windows, some of which turn out to be held together by a careful application of cellophane tape. One of the toilets is broken. The house came with an assortment of Post-it notes warning about chairs not to sit on and lamps that don't work. She keeps the clunky, black cordless phone — his from before they met — by her on the nightstand and sometimes even brings it with her in under the covers. She spends much of her at-home time *not* calling him. But then she'll forget, like the other morning when there was a deer outside the kitchen window, and she wanted him to know, only it was 4:30 a.m. in Arizona, and the man who answered wasn't her boyfriend, but rather a second-rate actor with a slow delivery who barely even knew his lines.

The first night of his visit, they make love standing up by the bedroom window, which looks out over the shadowy lacrosse field.

"Think anyone saw?" he asks, after.

"Are you kidding?" she says. "It will be a topic at the next faculty meeting."

Lying in bed beside her, he thinks of his room in Tucson, of the framed print of a hula dancer he can see from this very same position. It seems odd to be looking, now, at the outlines of an antique dresser. Kate kisses his chest and snuggles, then suddenly panics for a moment because she doesn't know where the phone is, and begins to track backward in her mind to the last time she used it. She remembers where she left it — the kitchen — at exactly the same moment she realizes it doesn't matter.

"I looked through the job list," she says. "There's something for you in Bemidji."

"Bemidji?" he says. "What the heck is Bemidji?"

"It's a place. You could get your ice fishing on. You could buy a truck with four-wheel drive."

"You want me to apply for this?"

"Of course," she says, not knowing if she does or doesn't. Lately, she doesn't believe half the things she hears herself say. Yesterday, she shouted at a kid, telling him that Billy Joel could wipe the floor with Dave Matthews any day of the week. "Wipe the floor" — she'd actually said that. She barely knows who Dave Matthews is. They were supposed to be translating Cicero. "You might as well."

"I have another year, if I want it. And they might do a search. And you hate the cold."

"They won't hire you. They never do. They always hire the other guy, the one they don't know. That's how it works."

"Then I'll move here."

"And do what?"

"Work in a bookstore."

"We don't have a bookstore. We have a cheese shop. You could work there. I stopped in the other day. They have four kinds of cheddar. It's like a Monty Python skit."

"I'll adjunct," he says. "Write my book. Start a band. Lighten up, will you?"

"Lighten up?" she says. "It's cold here, too. There are mice in the kitchen. There's a creep at the pool who wears a Speedo and times his laps to mine—he's married to a woman in English who looks like a stork. Do you understand? I'm afraid I'm going to take root here, like some lost seed. I'm afraid the next twenty years are going to sandbag me and I'll suddenly be her, just a character attached to this place, someone the students trade stories and speculate about over beers when they are on vacation in Positano."

"You think they'll hire you permanently?"

"I don't know. Maybe. You're missing the point."

Joe gives her a hug. "We have to be flexible," he says. "We're lucky we have jobs. All in all, things are going pretty well." Of the many girlfriends he's had over the years, Kate, whom he met two years ago in Iowa City when she nearly ran over him on her bicycle, is by far the most interesting; it has occurred to him that she should probably be on medication. Except then she might not be who she is, and what would be the point of that? The official story is that they now live together, here in Byron, even if he also has a place in Tucson. Temporary jobs require temporary homes.

"They are?" she says. "They're going well?" She's surprised by the sound of her own voice.

He finds it vaguely exciting that someone has been sneaking peeks at her underwater. He wraps his arms around her and kisses her ear, which he knows usually gets her going. It's practically an on-off switch.

She visits him next, a few weeks later, just before Thanksgiving, for which he'll be coming east. Instead of giggling sophomores poolside, she finds Joe hacking and running a low fever that won't go away. Still, he's game to show her around, and they hike to Finger Rock and drive out to the Desert Museum to see the hummingbirds, and she tries to be amusing and happy, but the color of his eyes is an alarming, wet pink, and he seems half-dead.

"Valley fever," he says, over chimichangas and margaritas in a popular, run-down Mexican restaurant in south Tucson, its outside walls decorated with hubcaps. "The doctor claims it has something to do with birds. The good thing is, you can only get it once. I'm all set for desert living from here on."

She stares at her silverware, none of which matches, and all of which seems to have come from Goodwill. She can't tell if this is quaint and authentic, or just someone's idea of quaint and authentic. His hair is getting overlong, and his skin has a greenish cast to it, in spite of all the sun he's been getting.

"Why are we together?" she asks. "Please tell me. Because I worry about it all the time."

"I don't know."

"You don't know? Do you think that's what I want to hear?"

He touches her hand. "*Telegamy*, remember?" This is a word he learned from her, one she may have invented. Things don't seem so bad if you have a name for them. His illness, for instance, which had him so down until he learned what it was called. To lay some groundwork in case he should get hired here permanently, he's already mentioned his "brilliant classicist" partner to at least three colleagues, one of whom turned out to be a senile professor emeritus — religion — who later tried to take his wallet. He had to physically push the man away.

"You like this. Displacement, setting up shop in a hostile, spiky environment." She's feeling it coming on again, the dark, nervous wash of energy that makes her misbehave, that makes her into, as her mother has always been so fond of pronouncing, "her own worst enemy." "And you know what?" she says. "It's not *telegamy*. Not really. Because if it were, we'd be married. *Monogamy, polygamy, telegamy*."

"You want me to marry you?" he asks.

"Oh, Jesus Christ. No. Absolutely not. I'm not ready for that. Nothing of the kind. I'd just like to try being in the same place for a while."

"Because I would."

"You would?" She looks down at her plate, at the shredded lettuce alongside the mangled remains of her meal. Her period is way overdue, she's been feeling strange, her breasts are sensitive. Last week, she bought a home testing kit, but it's back in upstate New York, still in its box. "You would?" she repeats. "That's nice of you."

Thinking about what he's just said, he feels suddenly dizzy. It occurs to him that he has in his defense the fact of his illness, which like drunkenness, or a pair of quotation marks, can serve to distance the apparent meaning of a statement from absolute or empirical truth. Of course, he would marry her. Given the right circumstances, he most certainly would. Maybe someday he will. He finishes his margarita and wonders about ordering them both another.

Thanksgiving is horrible — they spend most of it in the car. His uncle takes everyone out to a diner in New Jersey. This is supposed to be fun. The waitresses wear Pilgrim hats. On the ride back to Byron, she makes him pull over so she can throw up.

"It wasn't that bad," he says.

She thinks about how she didn't take her pills. About how she may have on purpose rolled the dice.

They don't talk about jobs at all.

At the Modern Language Association convention in Chicago, just after Christmas, she does not attend his paper. She couldn't care less about his paper. Joe has claimed not to have any interviews, but she's pretty sure he's cheating on her — not with a woman, but with a city in Minnesota. What she can't figure out is why he's keeping it a secret, inventing reasons he'll be gone for a while ("Coffee with Rob Skelton — you remember Rob . . ."). She's told him nothing. To tell him would be to influence the situation, and she doesn't want to do that. In *Star Trek* terms, she would be violating the Prime Directive, influencing the flow of history. Joe is a big *Star Trek* fan.

In the hotel lobby, where it is much more pleasant than the arctic air of room 1607 — the heat is out for their entire tower - - she watches the academics drift about with their coffees and their briefcases, eyes nervously darting around like those of prey on the veldt. She and Joe didn't even have Christmas this year. Instead, they have this — a convention. Restaurants, drinks (she's limited herself to one), more restaurants — she can barely fit into her good black pants. Tomorrow, they will each return to their respective homes. It worked out cheaper this way, and also, she's got an appointment at a clinic in Utica for Tuesday. She went back and forth on it, cried a little, called her friend Tonya back in Iowa, then chickened out and ended up making the whole conversation be about swimsuits and the impossibility of finding ones that didn't make them look like prudes or "before" advertisements for Weight Watchers. She's not that far gone. There probably isn't even a heartbeat yet. The temperature in Tucson at the moment, she happens to know, is sixty-two degrees. She's been monitoring it daily.

A young woman sits opposite her, pretty and also blonde, but with a face that's a little too pale, lips thin as French beans. She's wearing white hose under her charcoal skirt.

"God, I hate this," she says.

"Up for a job?" asks Kate.

She nods. Her skin is papery, her eyebrows barely there. "This is my third try. I defended two years ago. If I don't get something this year, I figure it's more or less over. I'm sorry, it's not your problem. But this is torture of a high order."

Kate squints to read the woman's convention badge, which announces that she is Dara Simeon, from Penn State. "Here's my advice, Dara. Pretend you're in court — answer all the questions, smile as much as you can, but don't offer information they don't specifically ask for. And don't say anything about your personal life, all right? You do *not* have a personal life."

"Thanks," she says, getting up and smoothing her skirt.

"You might want to imply you're sexually available," Kate says. "It couldn't hurt."

In the Hilton lobby, Joe waits for it to be time to ring up to the room and let them know he's here. He likes interviews, likes the feeling of possibility they provide. New people, new places. He's aware that Kate wants nothing more than to settle down and be done with it, and he appreciates that, but he's not sure he's there yet. It's a game they are playing, and he's always been good at games. People often underestimate him, and he likes that about himself. Even on the basketball court, he was always the surprise, the guy who could strip the ball from the opponent when he wasn't expecting it, head down for the easy layup. What she doesn't seem to understand is that he's *with* her. He is! This is how it works in academia. You sacrifice some things to gain others. If they were starting out as lawyers, they'd be working such long hours they'd never see each other anyway. If he were in the military, she'd have to get by with not seeing him for years at a time. He's tried to get her to see it his way, to understand that they have it better than everyone else. Two campuses, two different sets of friends.

He checks his watch. It's time. Bemidji? He doubts he'd go there under any circumstances. But this part, the dancing and dating, this part he can do. He's going to make them want him so bad they'll be sweating. The elevator doors hum and part. He's going to kill Bemidji.

She charms a guard and gains access to the book fair, wanders the tables and booths, marveling at the profluence of printed material, the sheer overwhelming weight of all this paper, of all these thoughts people have had. Textbooks and monographs and shiny novels and literary and scholarly journals. She should cancel the appointment, she thinks. This is not life. She could force herself to have one, a real one. The life of the mind is a lie. She first began studying Latin in high school, back in Des Moines, not because she liked it particularly, but because it made sense to her in a way that other things did not, things like boys, her lack of popularity, her father's silences, her mother's moods. With Latin, if you learned the rules, you were all set. You knew what was what. But then one thing had led to another, and now here she was. Had she ever wanted any of it? Her dissertation? The two years of teaching at a private school in Connecticut and coaching field hockey, a sport she barely understood but had lied about having played in order to get hired?

Another guard notices her lack of a convention badge and explains that she'll have to leave.

"It's all right," she says, brightly. "I'm in the wrong place anyway. I thought this was Marshall Field's."

Kate looks up at the thick snow sifting down out of the purple gray sky, visible through O'Hare's glass and steel exoskeleton. Joe's flight is delayed until at least 4:00 p.m. They are outside a coffee place, in between terminals. Already she can feel him slipping away. "I know about the interview," she says. "Just tell me how it went."

He looks into his cold coffee, then back up at her. "It was no big deal. I didn't want to upset you."

"Upset me? I told you about the job in the first place."

"Not so well. There were four of them in the room. One woman had huge tits, and I overcompensated and talked to a spot about a foot above her head." He coughs. All this is true. What he doesn't add is that on the way out, the chair of the search committee, a red-bearded man who looked like the descendent of lumberjacks, had shaken his hand, given him a meaningful look, and said, "You'll be hearing from us soon."

"Why would I want you not to interview? We need a real job, even if it does come with ice fishing."

"I never thought of it as real," he says. "But still, I shouldn't have kept it a secret."

Flights everywhere have been canceled, and people are hurrying past them in all directions, muttering, hauling their belongings, their tired children. Across from them, having beers at another table, is a couple who have obviously just returned from a cruise. They have tans, gold jewelry, hats. Kate understands that for some people, happiness is simply another commodity, that it absolutely can be purchased.

"Next week," she says, "if it isn't warm in Tucson, let's get in the car and drive south until we get someplace that is. Someplace with palm trees, all right?"

Joe sees on her face the hopeful, earnest expression he first fell in love with, the one that he's kept packed away in his mind and only taken out when he's thought that perhaps they should give up on this. Last week, she called him in tears to say that she'd made a fool of herself at a faculty party by leading everyone in a sing-along of "American Pie." "*I don't know what I'm supposed to be doing here,*" she'd said.

"Yes," he says. "That's exactly what we'll do."

"They're not the boss of us."

"No one is."

After they have kissed and said goodbye — their gates are in different terminals, and the weather is starting to let up — she walks slowly past the shops and hot dog stands, once again alone, and tries to stay calm by reminding herself of who she is. There is nothing like an airport terminal for this, for cutting identity down to its essentials. Job, home, destination, significant others. All of these people, temporarily cut loose from their moorings, scrambling to get back to someplace safe. Tomorrow, if only for a few days, she'll be back in the snowdrifts. *Modo fac!* she liked to say to her class on the first day of the semester, attempting to prove the flexibility and relevance of a dead language. *Just do it!* And this, her furious hands clacking chalk: *Hodie adsit, cras absit. Here today, gone tomorrow.* For a moment, she almost thinks she can hear him coming up behind her to tell her no, he's not going back, he's coming with her, and the hell with all of these people. But it's only one of those carts ferrying the elderly and overweight, and she hurries to get out of their way.

MAN UNDER

In mid-July, our landlady removed the front door to the house to get it repaired, and the next day, when I came back from my shift at Café D'Oro, the failing sandwiches-and-dessert place I'd managed to get hired at as a waiter, I discovered that we'd been robbed. The thieves had taken our black-and-white television and about two hundred dollars worth of stereo equipment. They'd also taken our instruments and amps.

Ed called Renata to yell at her. "How are we supposed to live with no door?" he asked. I sat at our tiny kitchen table and stared out over the clothes wires strung across the back yards. The wind was picking up and shaking the leaves and my skin felt clammy; a storm was coming in.

After a while, he came out of his bedroom and joined me. "What a bitch."

"I think she owes us money here," I said. "You can't take the door off a house in the middle of the city and not expect it to get robbed."

"She didn't want to talk about it. She says we have a door." This was true; the missing door was downstairs. The door to our apartment was still in place, though the wood in the frame around the strike plate was all busted out where the thieves had kicked their way through. Ed took out a Viceroy from his shirt pocket and went into the kitchen to light it off a burner. He'd recently cut his long hair and grown a goatee, hung up photos of Charles Mingus and Ron Carter on his bedroom wall. He'd been wearing the same suit jacket over a series of white T-shirts now for more than a month. "She said she was disappointed in us."

"She's going to be a lot more disappointed now that we have no equipment." I looked around. Husks of dirty paint curled down from the ceiling near the windows. A narrow hall led to the front bedroom, which served as Ed's room and our rehearsal area. We'd hung up one of those Indian drug-curtain things on a clothesline to separate the entrance to my tiny room off his, in which I barely had space for a single bed, a dresser, and a chair. We had this place at a below-market rate because we'd promised to make a lot of noise. The landlady wanted the old man downstairs to move out of his rent-controlled unit, and she figured we might do the trick.

"I'm reporting to you what she said."

"Maybe she ought to just give us a couple of thousand to kill him," I said. "It's simpler."

"I'll suggest it. She says if something doesn't happen relatively soon, she's raising the rent."

"*Relatively?*"

"Her word."

"She was going to raise it anyway, right? I mean, eventually?"

"I guess." He flexed his hands, picked at a bit of callus that was flaking off.

"So let's not worry too much about her. We've got a lease." Something about the way he didn't look at me obviated the next question, but I asked anyway. "We do have a lease, right?"

"Not exactly. More like an understanding." For all his competence — as a musician, a world-class partier, a guy who had rebuilt a TR-6 when he was only sixteen — Ed still often displayed a certain inability to peer around the sides of things to see what else might be there.

"An *understanding?*"

"We shook hands and all."

"So she could put us out tomorrow?"

"Oh, I don't think so. There are laws about such things. Look at the guy downstairs."

"But she can take our front door off."

"It's her door." He got more of the skin. "Maybe the police will find those fucks."

"You think?" I'd asked the officer who responded to our 911 call what the likelihood of our getting our stuff back was, and he'd looked at me like I'd asked if I might borrow his gun for a day or two.

"Those amplifiers were heavy. It had to be more than one person. A team. Plus, what the hell went on? I mean, that took a couple of trips. I think this was a planned heist."

I stared at the spot where the television used to be. "There's really no lease?" I was going to miss watching Dan Rather do the evening news. Harry Chapin had just died. They'd found the guy who was killing all those people in Atlanta. England was gearing up for the royal wedding.

"Look at it this way. No lease is *way* more rock and roll."

Ed had found this place for us in anticipation of my arrival. For the past year, he'd been living in a rented room in Jamaica, Queens. Growing up in New Jersey, I'd visited Manhattan many times, but I'd never been across the river. The word *Brooklyn* itself seemed strung with high-tension cable to me — written down, it even looked a little like a bridge. I'd driven down from college in Maine the month before, smoking Old Golds the whole way, in a boxy Fiat 128 I'd bought off a guy with a sharpening business in Skowhegan for fifteen hundred dollars my parents had fronted me. It was more of a toy than a car, with cheap plastic stick controls coming out of the steering column and gasoline smell leaking from the cloth-covered engine hoses — but I pretended it was a Porsche, the windows rattling in the doors, reflections of the East Coast screening across my Ray-Bans: Portland, Providence, Hartford, New Haven. I had two thousand dollars my grandmother had given me for graduation, and a red Gibson SG Special that shone like a waxed apple. When

I ran it through my Sunn amp with the two twelve-inch Celestions and hit the 20x switch on the front, I could deafen passing birds at a hundred yards, tree squirrels, and make the neighborhood Dobermans whimper.

Most of the brownstones on our block, like ours, were pretty decrepit. Cracks ran across them, and there were occasional missing hunks of lintel and broken steps. Many still had working gas lights out front, and at night the street probably looked a lot like it had a hundred years earlier. The wave of gentrification was coming this way — you could see it in the distrustful faces of the local residents, mostly older folks, Italian and Irish, as they watched us come and go, wondering what we were up to. They were right to wonder. Rehearsing a band was, apparently, legal, so long as we knocked off by 10:00 p.m. I had never seen our downstairs neighbor, although there were things I'd noticed. He was a smoker, and often a late-night whiff of cigarette traveled up from his apartment and into ours. Also, he liked watching Johnny Carson — I could hear that, too, through the holes in the floor around my radiator.

We went to two pawnshops thinking that we might find our stuff there, but it was hopeless. So, we bought replacement equipment, used, on Forty-eighth Street, in the city. It took most of the rest of my savings. I got a battered Melody Maker and fifty-watt Music Man amp. Ed found an old Ampeg tube amp with a foldout top, and a Fender Precision with what looked like a bullet hole near the bridge. He stuck lit cigarettes in there while he played. Renata grudgingly agreed to pay for a locksmith, who came and installed a new deadbolt on our apartment door. The building still had no front door, and from the sidewalk you could see right up the front stairs, but at least there was something for us to lock at night. Neighborhood cats came in and out freely. So did a number of pigeons.

We invited over Greeny Greenburg, a drummer I'd met down at

the café who was in his thirties, and this Filipino guy named Jet that Ed knew from his work up in the Garment District. Jet was short, with medium-length hair, and a round, pleasant face. His big, tinted, aviator-style glasses made him seem more like he should have been assembling model airplanes than playing music, and his Gibson Explorer looked huge hanging off him — he wore it so low that one of the corners nearly brushed the tops of his sneakers. He sent his left hand on a nimble tour of the fretboard, low to high, then back low again, the distortion-coated notes coming fast and thick as bees. It was the fastest I'd ever heard anyone play anything.

"Damn," I said.

Ed grinned. "Do that again."

Jet did it again, more or less identically.

"He's a prodigy," said Ed. "His first instrument was clarinet."

Jet was expressionless. For all his obvious gifts, he looked more like what he was — an accounts receivable clerk — than a rock star. "You guys know Foghat?" he asked. "'Slow Ride'?" His voice was reedy and thin.

"Foghat?" I said. I looked at Ed, my partner, Lennon to my Mc-Cartney, the guy who'd tutored me in music appreciation all through high school, from showing me what was good about the Beach Boys and how to sing harmony, to introducing me to George Duke and Chick Corea. He might have been turning into a beatnik, but he still had taste when it came to rock. He knew the difference between quality music and the junk they turned out for teenagers to wave their lighters to.

But he just shrugged. "So long as it's loud."

Greeny's eyes went misty with anticipation. "I can be loud," he said.

"We can be loud and good at the same time," I pointed out.

It turned out to be a Foghat night. After "Slow Ride," we played "I

Just Want to Make Love to You." That was pretty much it; we played each of them at concert length and then some. We played them loud enough that my ears began to feel they'd been stuffed with peanut butter and then blown at with a hair dryer. We played them in the same key, which was even more torturous, for the simple reason that "Slow Ride" and "I Just Want to Make Love to You" are almost exactly the same song. Jet soloed, I soloed, Ed soloed, Greeny soloed. We went around again. It was like bidding in a never-ending, ridiculously loud poker game. We played these songs and then, just to be sure we really had them down, we played them again. When it was all over and we were packing up, the silence that filled the apartment had a tactile quality, like cotton batting.

Ed and I took a couple of beers up the ladder to the roof and stood looking out toward the city. This was the great thing about our apartment — we could see the Statue of Liberty from up there, and the World Trade Center, floating in the distance above the solid but unremarkable brownstones and warehouses.

"The guy's probably deaf or something," I said. "He didn't even bang on the floor."

"Or something." Ed shook his head in sympathy.

"I'm not paying double for this apartment."

"How about we get some power tools up here and saw through a television?"

"We don't *have* a television anymore." I kicked at a loose piece of mortar that had fallen from our chimney. "But maybe that's it," I said, growing philosophical. "We have to pursue badness as a form of art. We need to expand the frontiers of ugly."

"Could be he's a Foghat fan." Ed stroked the newly sprouted hairs on his chin.

"Do you see what I'm saying?" I went on. "It's ironic. Here's this thing we want more than anything, to play music, and the only way we're going to be able to keep on doing it is if we do it really badly."

A motorcycle coughed and spat its way up the block, hesitated at the stop sign on the corner, then shot angrily onto the next street.

"Alice is pushing hard for me to move in with her," he said. "Her roommate is going to California."

"When?"

"Like yesterday."

"That's a terrible idea," I said. Ed and Alice — an actual cheer-leader — had started dating our senior year of high school. I couldn't believe they were still together — Alice didn't even like music. She was living on the Upper East Side and working for Drexel Burnham. She came over on weekends, which I really hated — I didn't like how Ed changed when she was around, how he seemed always on stage and overanimated. "I mean, not that you asked."

"You know how she answers the phone at her office?" he said. "'Money desk.' It's like she's sitting there on top of some huge pile of coins."

"She is. She told me. She said she likes the way it feels."

"Coins, or bills?"

"Coins, I think. Krugerrands or something."

"Hell, man," he said. "I'm not moving anywhere."

"All I'm saying is you should think about what you're commit-ting to."

I could see his features in the dim light, and they had hardened and become more adult. I thought I could imagine what he'd look like at forty. "I think you're missing the point anyway," he said. "Bad isn't the issue. Loud is. The guy isn't a music critic. To him loud *is* bad."

"You do what you have to do," I said. "We're not married or any-thing."

"I got us a gig," Greeny said to me over his plate of eggs, scrambled, soft, with rye toast. It was slow this morning, like every morning, so I hovered by his table while he ate. "Out in the Hamptons." Greeny had a job in the city selling off-brand personal computers. Every morning he came in for the same breakfast, dressed in a sport coat and slacks. He always tipped the same, too, a single dollar bill, which actually made him a big spender. I'd gone over to his place once to pick up forty dollars worth of pot — his other profession was small-time dealer — and I'd met his girlfriend, a bruised-looking brunette who'd come to the door to let me in wearing sweatpants and a man's shirt open in the front to reveal a lacy pink bra. She left the room while Greeny and I talked, and I wondered if after I left he was going to go back to beating her.

"Really?" I said.

"One of those beach houses full of yuppies. Five hundred. You in?"

"What did you tell them we play?"

"Everything, man. Fifties, sixties." He took a final bite of eggs. "You want to know what we're called?"

I did.

He held his hands up, framing the air in front of him. "'Brooklyn.' Like 'Boston,' right? I don't think anyone else is using it yet."

I looked out the window. Across the street, in front of the new Korean market that had just supplanted an Irish bar, two cars were engaged in a game of chicken over a parking place. The paired notes of their horns was, I noted, a perfect tritone.

He crunched some toast. He was really pleased with this. "I knew you'd like it," he said.

That afternoon, an old guy came into the café, sat down at a table by the window and ordered coffee. I brought it to him, along with a little pitcher of milk. I went back to reading the paper at the table nearest the counter. He was the only person in the place. The café did almost no business, and as a job, it was pretty much a joke, but I did get to eat a meal — anything I wanted on the menu. Olivia, the Greek woman who cooked, seemed to enjoy making me food. It gave her something to do.

After a while, I went over to check on him.

"Milk," he said, tapping the creamer, which I saw was empty. I took it away and got Olivia to refill it, then brought it back to him. I went back to my paper. I'd been going through the Help Wanted ads. There wasn't anything I felt qualified to do. I wondered what you had to have studied in school to get appointed to the Money Desk.

I went to check on him again. "More coffee?" I asked.

"More milk."

The creamer was empty. His coffee cup was just about empty too, other than a puddle of light brown at the bottom — if he filled it again he was going to be drinking straight milk. Which, it suddenly occurred to me, was the point. The guy was drinking as much milk as he could for the price of a cup of coffee. Still, I had Olivia give me another refill.

Another half hour went by. It was raining out, although lightly. No one else had come in. Our selection of Italian pastries — delivered on Tuesdays and not thrown away until the following Monday — glowed preternaturally in their glass case by the register. I went to bring him the check.

He studied it briefly, then tossed it to the table. "Sorry," he said. The bone structure of his face was evident under his skin, and I thought he probably had been a pretty good-looking man in his day. He had straight gray hair, a full head of it, even at his age, which had to be past seventy. His blue-green eyes looked murky, and I wondered if he saw very well out of them.

"You don't have seventy-nine cents?"

He shook his head.

On the one hand, I felt bad for him. This was a pretty pathetic way to fill up your stomach. But I represented the café right now, and the café was being wronged. "You can't do stuff like this," I said. "You can't just go into a place and order food that you don't have money to pay for."

"Sure, I can," he said. "I just did."

"Well, I mean, you *can*. But you're not supposed to."

"Why not?"

"Come on. You know why not. The social contract. The rules. The world doesn't work that way. Things cost money."

"Let me ask you something. That coffee I drank — it was already made, right? It was sitting in a pot, just cooking away on a burner." He gestured toward where our two Pyrex containers of coffee sat waiting. "After a while, it gets bitter and nasty tasting. What are you going to do with it? You're going to throw it out. That being the case, and business being what it is" — he gestured around at the empty room — "you can afford to give me a cup of coffee. In fact, maybe it's your duty to do it. If you've got something you don't want, and you throw it away rather than give it so someone who does want it, that's not just wrong, it's spiteful." He dug briefly in his nostril with his pinky. "You're one of them from the third floor."

For a moment, I considered pretending I had no idea what he meant, but I could see that this wouldn't work — he had me fixed in his gaze now, and I felt even worse about lecturing him on the coffee. "Sorry about all the noise," I said.

"I heard worse," he said. "I fought in Sicily. Try the sound of an eight-inch howitzer sometime."

The conversation seemed to have reached an impasse. "You want a cannoli?" I asked.

"For free? Or for money. Because I just told you, I don't have any."

"For free. Or on me, anyhow. For the trouble about the apartment."

"Those things are nearly a week old. I'm down around here a lot. I see how often the delivery guy comes. No thanks."

"All right," I said. "I'm going to let you slide on the seventy-nine cents. But you have to understand that not everyone else is going to be this easy to deal with."

"It makes you feel good to say that, doesn't it? You'll let me slide."

"I don't feel one way or the other."

"Then forget about that slide part. Make it that you gave me a cup of coffee. That's a nice thing. You can feel good about it, I can feel good about it. We're neighbors, after all."

"Fine," I said, taking his cup away. "I hope you enjoyed your coffee."

"Not much," he said. "But thanks for asking."

The beach house was in Quogue. We got there around 4:00 p.m. and set up in the living room. People in robes and swimsuits passed through, some nodding at us, though it was clear they thought we were about as interesting as plumbers called in to fix the toilets. At five, the drinking started in earnest, and by six there were attractive, tanned Manhattanites everywhere, sipping wine, drinking bottles of Heineken, slipping off to the bathroom to do lines. We partied with them, or tried to. Partied around them might better describe it, as they seemed not to notice us at all.

I was determined to break through to the other, beautiful side. "What about those air traffic controllers?" I said to a surprised-looking woman with dark hair and bright red lipstick.

"I think they're idiots," she said. She sized me up, then apparently decided not to eat me. "They're overpaid as it is. The president is doing exactly the right thing."

"Not exactly standing with the working man, huh?"

"Are *you* a working man?"

"No," I admitted. "But that's not for lack of trying."

"Excuse me," she said, "but are you supposed to be here? I mean, do you know someone from the house?"

"I know you," I said.

"That's probably not sufficient. This is a private house."

"I'm with the band."

She brightened. "The band! I heard there was going to be a band. Well, then, that's all right. What do you play?"

"Do you like Foghat?"

"I don't know," she said. "I might."

"Don't you think Reagan is a little, I don't know, creepy?" I asked. "Like someone who'd try to sell you stuff on late night TV?"

"You might not think it to look around, but about half of us here at the house are Republicans."

"But you're cool with drugs."

"Way cool," she said. "What have you got?"

We played for them, and they danced. They danced and waved their hands in the air and drank and smoked, and the air filled with the scent of sweat and ocean, and there was sand all over the wooden floors. We were one strange band. Greeny had brought along a gold-toothed Jamaican guy named Dave King to our last couple of rehearsals, and we now had "Jammin'" and "No Woman No Cry" and "Many Rivers to Cross" in our repertoire, which also comprised a couple of rockabilly numbers, a version of Steely Dan's "Bodhisattva," and — at Ed's insistence — a rendition of Coltrane's "Impressions." Dave King knew almost none of the lyrics to his reggae songs, but it didn't matter because he wore a colorful floppy hat, had a nice voice and great accent, and was happy to rap away for as long as you'd let him about "Jah" and "one love," and whatever. He was a hit ("Where did you find him?" my surprised-looking Republican asked me during one of the breaks), even though I suspected a lot of the time even *he* didn't know what he was saying. He passed around a big splif during "Jammin'." We stopped at 1:00 a.m., but the yuppies took up a collection and presented us with another hundred bucks and we played an extra hour, finishing up with "Slow Ride," for what had to have been the fourth time. I felt unstable, unreal. "Slow ride!" the bankers and brokers shouted along with us, positioned in front of us like figures in a bacchanal. "Take it easy!"

On the same day that our front door finally reappeared — now painted a glossy black — I got a job proofreading tombstone ads for a publisher on Wall Street. Café D'Oro had closed — I showed up for work one day and the place was locked up tight. Ed had found a gig accompanying a piano player at Top of the Sixes, where the full windows next to the urinals in the men's room allowed a dizzying view down onto the city streets. He'd be moving shortly; I'd already put up signs down at Key Food to try and find another roommate. The rich, we agreed, really are different from the rest of us — they even peed differently. Tombstones are those big notices in the financial pages that announce, for instance, new issues of bonds, followed by literally hundreds of names of various corporate underwriters. My job was to sit alone in a small office with these things spread out in front of me, going back and forth between the originals and the ones that would be appearing in the paper, looking for mistakes, of which there were almost never any. Once I found "Salomon" spelled "Solomon." After a couple weeks of squinting and giving myself headaches, I began to realize that I didn't need to try so hard. I started skimming over the stuff without really looking at all. I began to hope I was missing stuff; getting fired would be just fine with me.

On the subway home one evening, my train shuddered to a halt short of a station and the lights went out. We sat in darkness for a while, all of us strangers continuing to pretend that we had nothing to do with one another, that we weren't suddenly part of something larger than ourselves. Invisible newspapers shifted and rustled, throats were cleared. Then the engineer's distorted voice came over the intercom: "Motorman, we have a man under."

We'd hit someone. I felt my pulse race. Somewhere out there, perhaps only yards away, separated from our little car of commuters by a thin layer of steel and glass, was tragedy. Life and death. We waited. I smelled cologne, a vague hint of mothballs, a growing scent of sweat. *Man under.* We continued to wait. Lights flashed outside the windows, there were mysterious sounds, shouts, clanks. We weren't responsible, and yet we couldn't go — this was our tragedy, like it or not. Minutes passed and still no one spoke. Then, with no further comment from the conductor, the lights flickered back on, there was a whirring sound of engines coming to life. The car jolted like it had been kicked from behind, sighed once, and proceeded forward.

ANOTHER COYOTE STORY

By about the fourth somersault I knew I had no chance of surviving. A bouncing, limp puppet, I'd lost skis, poles, hat, gloves, glasses. Every now and then, in the tiny intervals when the ten guys in boots who were kicking me in the ribs stopped to catch their breath, I thought I saw the sky. My mind slowed way down the way it used to on rainy afternoons in math class back in high school — voices of smokers and lovers floating up from the parking lot, the wind shaking the leaves of the big oak just outside the window, the inscrutable geometry of my future a momentary stop against time — and I weighed various endings. If I didn't hit a tree, it would be a rock. That, the exposed nut of my head meeting an unforgiving bit of landscape, would be sudden, and probably the thing to hope for. I also imagined sailing over a cliff, a more exhilarating, spectacular end (surely, people were watching this), but one that might allow too much time for thought. I blew snow from my mouth — it kept accumulating — and tried to tell if my neck was broken yet (I didn't think so). I heard a loud "huh, huh" sound, wondered what it was, then realized that I was the one making it and that I was hyperventilating, this perhaps in response to having the wind knocked out of me repeatedly at regular half-second intervals. Then, with no particular sense of failure or accomplishment — really, with no sense of *event* at all — it was over. How did it feel? The nearest I can come is leaving the house and suddenly remembering you left your keys. Like that.

You expect crepe, relatives, a fiery transition from material form, possibly some sort of tunnel of blue light. I was taken out to steak night at The Lion and Turtle.

The undergraduate to my right was angry. Sherman Alexie had

apparently bailed at the last minute, and I was his sub. "I read all his books," she said, tucking her brown hair back behind her ears. "I was so stoked to meet him."

There were six of us around the table, working on our waters and a big basket of bread. I didn't want to say anything, because I was pretty sure I'd bitten my tongue through in about nine places, and if I opened my mouth, I was likely to disgorge a fair gob-full of blood. Instead, I reached into the basket and removed a roll.

"What do you plan to read tonight?" asked a man about my own age, with a preposterously black goatee, black turtleneck, black jacket, and black plastic-rimmed glasses. It was immediately clear to me that if he hadn't yet had an affair with the student who had been so stoked, they were on the verge of it. They had a way of ignoring each other so thoroughly you just knew they were involved.

Now, in my life, I should say, I was sort of a writer. I wrote catalog copy, mostly, for universities and small colleges. "Nestled in the heart of scenic central Pennsylvania, St. Lawrence College of Scranton provides an exceptional value in undergraduate education." "Baltimore Union, an exciting urban university — let's grow together!" And sure, like every third person you meet, I'd started my share of novels, never getting much more than fifteen pages into them before realizing that I was out of ideas, that my plot consisted more or less of what had happened to me that day, and that in lieu of any real plan, I just kept making up new characters — an outward, rather than forward motion. So perhaps all of that had been some kind of sin — vanity? — and this was my punishment. In any event, I was stuck. These people wanted me to perform.

I sipped my water, stalling for time. Something about the faces of the people around me suggested I might be in the middle west, or close anyway — perhaps Ohio. The salads that arrived were entirely iceberg.

"Something from the new book?" suggested the formerly stoked girl. I nodded. That sounded as good as anything. She had nice eyes.

I probed my mouth with my tongue; as far as I could tell, I wasn't hemorrhaging, and the teeth were all there.

The professor — he had to be one, even if he'd been drawn by a cartoonist — buttered a roll. "Do you get to New York much? I'd kill to spend an hour in a real bookstore, get a decent cup of coffee. You know what I'm talking about. Culture out here is a bunch of white women meeting once a week to discuss *Beloved*, which they haven't read and couldn't if they tried, but they do get to drink a little blush wine and eat cheese, so it's worth it."

His students, I thought, seemed a little tired of him.

"As a Native American writer," a skinny boy across the table from me asked, his voice the timbre of a badly played oboe, "do you ever feel compelled to address certain subject matter that you might otherwise not? In other words, is your identity controlling, or liberating?" He colored visibly, his pale skin growing blotchy. "I hope that wasn't out of line."

The thing we don't know about death is how sarcastic it makes you. The dead understand life in a remarkably hard, scientific light — none of that weepy, Raphael-angels-and-Mozart stuff the living want to project on us. From the outside, life tends to look like an elaborate setup for a joke. Think Rube Goldberg, think banana peels. Quite the opposite of how it feels when you are in it: it's clear, linear, unsentimental as mathematics. In my case, my thumpy exit was the sum of the following, in reverse order:

Choosing to follow my buddy Rick onto a narrow, steeply pitched ski slope boiled over with big moguls that had frozen overnight and made a sound like a cat hissing if you tried to turn on one, which I did, unsuccessfully.

Smoking a fat joint on the chairlift with Rick's stoner friend, Josh, on the way up, before my first run, still hung over and tired from a long day of skiing the day before (not to mention the whole business with the fire alarms), and way out of practice with dope smoking anyway.

Putting on the new bib-style ski pants I'd purchased specifically for this trip, which had the effect of turning me into a kind of greased bullet as I caromed down that slope in the Utah morning, actually *picking up* speed as I went rather than slowing, my occasional attempts to turn face down and legs downhill (self-arrest!) useless against the gravity that had me putting on a tumbling act.

Going on this trip at all.

The further back you go, the less obvious connections become, but that doesn't mean they aren't there. A half mile short of Niagara Falls (U.S. side, Bridal Veil), there is water that appears to be just standing around minding its own business. "You don't know what you're in for!" Cleo shouted at it, when we visited just last year. We'd been fighting again, though we weren't just then. "I have seen your future, and it's not pretty!"

But of course, it was. I bought her a souvenir rainbow mug.

Three fire trucks. Me, standing out in the Utah night with at least one hundred other perturbed ski vacationers. "It's nothing," I'd told the blonde girl at the front desk a few minutes earlier. "You can turn it off." She couldn't. New hotel. Manager off the premises. An air-horn sound banging through all of our brains at one-second intervals, just in case anyone should forget that this was an emergency. Bells ringing, too.

Chickens. Three of them (one per truck? — patterns emerge only in retrospect), pierced repeatedly and strategically, garlic shoved into the holes. I pointed out the smoke that was beginning to creep from the stove burners, white wisps of it, fragrant, but just a little foul smelling too (no pun). "We'll open a window," said Martin. He and I had been hired together back in Colorado. His gig was computers, mine PR. On weekends we'd pick a ski area and drive to it. A former rugby player, he was well over two hundred pounds and skied in a greenish oilskin affair that came down to the knees and was more the kind of thing you'd wear trout fishing in the Highlands. He'd been married in a kilt — I'd seen the photos. "Air things out a bit." When the room started to get really smoky and our detector began to beep, someone else had the bright idea of opening the door to the hallway, too, to get a little cross-ventilation.

Seven exhausted, hungry guys in their forties crammed into a two-bedroom suite, every inch of the floor taken up with clothes, boots, sleeping bags, mattress pads. A couple of beers, someone rolls a joint. Grocery bags arrayed on the countertop and the small kitchen table, chips and jars of supermarket-brand salsa. The other guys were married, but I still wasn't, and it was starting to feel embarrassing. The art on the walls was tasteful in an invisible way — pastels, flowers — there mostly to remind you that this was a *quality* room. Cheaper hotel, uglier art. Fly in first class and you get a free drink and a different kind of tray table, but it's still the same plane. Our window had a good view of the parking lot and a few office buildings, dark mountains looming in the distance behind them.

In the restaurant's bathroom, I attempted to put my hand through the sink, but met resistance in exactly the form one would expect. Death did not preclude pain, nor did it apparently come with any of the expected benefits — I could not pass through things, read minds, or see the future. Even the past was a little hazy. The present, this cinnamon-scented men's room, was all too real. When I was eleven, I sent away for X-ray specs, which never came. Probably better that way. At the Community Park Pool I stared at the girls in their suits, thinking *when I get those glasses*, never knowing that I had just made my first foray into victimhood and the marketplace. "Eastern Illinois State — discover your future!" So now I tried to determine whether it was just me that had died, or whether the whole bunch of us were translated. Perhaps Sherman Alexie was the one lucky member of this doomed party — Waylon Jennings opting not to take the plane at the last moment and giving his seat to the Big Bopper — and we were all of us dead. Had my dining companions, too, been in Utah? Did it matter? Maybe when it happened, you just went to Ohio, period. I checked my face in the mirror, recognized it, saw nothing particularly Native American in the features. No visible blood, either. My ribs, however, hurt with every breath.

A perfectly pleasant day of winter sport yesterday on which I did not die. Why would I? I was forty, just turned. I was not nearly so sarcastic, the opposite, even. I rode high above those sugared cliffs and gorges, gulped distinctly western air, and thought about how certain moments can be relived. Or rather, there are places one can return to that have nothing to do with outside circumstance or chronological context. Sex. The beach. The shower. Chocolate. Listening to *Sgt. Pepper's* with your eyes closed, feet up. Floating unnaturally above the world on a metal bench, looking down through a pair of skis. I'd never been there, and yet I'd been there so many times I felt like slapping myself on the back: *Dude! Where you been? We missed you!* I thought backward from there to other ski moments. The weekend trips to A-Basin with Martin. A trip with Cleo to Vermont that proved beyond any doubt my unreasonableness, when I left her at the bottom and skied the blacks all day because it was why I had come. And yet we moved in together anyway, that next year, and she dutifully bought me calendars with mountain scenes on them every December.
    And back, and back.

Dinner went as well as could be hoped, considering I was faking it all the way. Luckily, no one wanted to ask me anything specific — they seemed to respect my privacy as a Native American writer filling in for a Native American writer. Since I was a backup, it occurred to me that expectations were probably lower. Still, there was going to be the reading part of the evening, and that worried me. I asked if anyone had my book, and was surprised to discover that the blotchy boy did. Coffee had come — for my meal I'd opted for the steak, which was overcooked and sided with a baked potato jacketed in foil — along with a "special" dessert for all of us, a precarious piece of chocolate cake with a layer of something red just beneath the icing.

Lucky Sherman Alexie. He hadn't fallen off the side of some mountain.

"Do you actually know Sherman Alexie?" asked the girl. Her name, predictably, was Heather. I wondered if the rules were that everyone got to hear my thoughts.

"No, not exactly."

"I think he's wonderful. But I was so angry when I heard he wasn't coming that you know what? I called his mother."

Everyone at the table seemed to think this was hilarious. Apparently, the story was familiar to them. "How?"

"I found the number, right there on the rez, and I called. She was very nice. I just said how disappointed I was — that's all. She said she'd let him know."

I could tell how much she enjoyed saying *rez*.

"Can I see it?" I asked the boy.

"I was hoping you'd sign it." He dug into the knapsack that he'd apparently had tucked between his feet through the whole meal. "Here."

Had my parents (or I) been alive, I'd have called them. There in my hands was a hardbound book with my name on it. It was remarkable. I started to flip through, but from the leaving motions taking place around me I determined it was time to go. There *were* people I needed to call. My dentist, for instance, was expecting me on Wednesday, and that wasn't going to happen. And Cleo.

I took the pen the boy held out and wrote my name on the title page. The book seemed to be called *Zip*. I tried to figure the significance of this. *Zip* as in *pep*? As in zippo, zilch, nothing? Was it a message? I could not for the life of me (hah!) remember writing it.

They drove me to a small auditorium and I did the reading. It was easy. My book was full of stories, and I just chose one. There were about twenty people in the audience. It was a Coyote story, all about how Coyote was hanging out on a big flat rock one day, when Lizard came by to ask directions. The characters all called each other "Grandfather" and "Uncle," and I didn't understand a word of it. Things happened, characters went places, had cryptic conversations, then moved on to other places. Big winds kicked up, rains came and went, talking animals were tricked into doing things. People applauded. They took me to a motel a few miles from campus and I watched TV and went to bed.

After that reading, I did more, at other small colleges, driving myself to them in a tiny rental car, using a handout map of Ohio with "Thrifty" printed across the top and directions to the Columbus airport on the reverse. I read other stories from my book, but I didn't understand them any better than that first one. I began to think I'd written a very good book — like life, it had the appearance of meaning, but at the same time, the harder you worked at looking under the surface, the more the whole thing just dissolved before you. At a highway trading post, I bought myself a belt with a turquoise-inlaid buckle. I tried to decide which reservation I might be from.

Sometimes, I'd stare at those directions back to the airport and wonder if there was a simple way out for me in them. Perhaps I should ignore the itinerary — it was printed on letterhead from my publisher, Zip Books — and just head home. Except that I knew what would happen. Surely that plane would take me back to Utah, and then I'd be right back where I'd started, which is to say dead on a frozen hillside, surrounded by a chastened group of men who just the evening before had found it hilarious to have emptied an entire hotel of its guests with three chickens and some garlic.

Of course, at each successive stop, there was disappointment. Everyone had been hoping for Sherman Alexie. I got used to it. They put me up in local hotels, many of which had free HBO. I tried to telephone Cleo, but always got an answering machine. My name was not mentioned, and that led me to believe that time had moved on more than I knew. I ate Ibuprofen like M&M's, four every three hours, and drank as much as I felt like, despite what I'd read in the magazines about liver damage. I recognized some of the schools I visited as ones I'd written copy for. "Ohio Lutheran, where the future is now!" There was a sameness to all of them — the students in their baseball caps, the professors eager to meet me, the visiting dead writer. During question-and-answer time at the end of a reading, I'd often be asked specific things. Is Grasshopper the hero of that story, or is it Grandfather Owl? What was the significance of the sweat lodge? At first, I'd answer honestly that I did not know, but my honesty was taken for cageyness. After a while, I started answering questions with questions. What do you think? I'd say. Not all stories are linear, I'd tell them.

An unexpected bump up to first class, where I drank Bloody Marys as quickly as the stewardess (sorry, attendant, but now you know her gender) could bring them. Thinking to myself, *You are so lucky.*

Sliding all over the interstate trying to get myself from Utica, where we now lived, to the Syracuse airport in a blizzard, praying I wouldn't land in a ditch and miss my flight and the thing I'd been training daily at the gym for, planning my life around, to the exclusion of almost anything else. To the point where Cleo pretty much stopped talking to me at all — I mean, I was executing jump-turns in the kitchen of our tiny rental house, causing the dishes to shake in the cabinets. Turning off the radio for less distraction and leaning way forward to see through the flakes.

I ate, but I was always hungry; I drank, but I never got drunk. Steaks, chops, great huge sandwiches and desserts, martinis and margaritas and straight-up Scotch. I even took up smoking again. What did it matter? I'd lived with the woman for seven years, and now I couldn't even get her on the telephone. It occurred to me that none of this might be happening at all, that in fact I might still be lying on the snow like a broken toy. *Nice turn.*

Her father was sick, so we moved to Utica. It was a nice thing to do, I suppose. He lingered for over a year; I telecommuted. Cleo looked tired all the time, and maybe we fell out of love, or maybe we just stopped trying to tell *our* story.

Finally, at a small alternative college — there really are a lot of colleges in Ohio — a young man in a cape was assigned to show me around. He had the usual multiple facial piercings and a speech impediment from the silver ball imbedded in the center of his tongue. "Do you *know* Therman Alexie?" he asked.

"Oh, we all know each other," I said. We were headed across the main quadrangle. The buildings were of gray stone, planted two hundred years earlier by earnest Unitarians intent on civilizing the frontier. A couple of girls in oversized dresses played a lackluster game of Frisbee, both of them with cigarettes in their hands. "I want to go up there," I said, pointing to the clock tower. "I'll bet there's even a legend about it."

"Thatth right," he said. "It will thtrike thirteen — "

"The day a virgin graduates."

"How'd you know?"

"Lucky guess."

"Ith a joke, man. The women here want you to thign a contract before you hold their handth. That thing ought to thtrike thirteen every night."

I got him to take me up — he had a big key ring with keys to all the buildings. We went out on the balcony overlooking the quad. It was dark already, and nearly time to head back to my room and change for dinner. The girls had given up on their game.

"What do you write?" I asked the boy.

"Poetry, mothtly. I can't theem to tell a thtory. Fiction ith boring anyway."

"I'll bet you've got something to say. I'll bet you're really talented, but just too unusual for the world to understand your talent. You're misunderstood, aren't you, cape-boy?"

"Are you being tharcathtic?" he asked. "And if tho, how come? What did I do to you?"

"Nothing," I said. "I was just checking." And then I climbed up onto the railing and swan-dived toward the concrete below.

This fall wasn't much like the last. For one thing, it was over in a second. Just a graceful suspension, then the hard smack of the ground. No time to think, in other words, which was just as well. I didn't want to think. I didn't want to know what would happen if, for instance, I tried to ditch my responsibilities in a less dramatic way and simply steal away to the Columbus airport.

That morning I'd arisen early, intending to leave her sleeping there, but she'd beaten me to it, and the coffee was already going downstairs. I put on my robe and clumped down to where she was sitting at the table in the predawn, knocking snow off the morning paper, which had somehow made it to our doorstep. "I'll miss you," she'd said. "Even though you're abandoning me."

And I kissed her on the top of her sleep-smelling head and didn't say anything, because I never did, but instead just began assembling my bags.

I don't know who they got to replace me.

JIMI HENDRIX, BLUEGRASS STAR

In front of the Pompidou Center, a pretty redheaded girl with a violin case took a position about fifteen yards to my left. She wore tight jeans and a black cowboy shirt with pearly buttons, and I kept one eye on her as she took out her instrument and applied rosin to the bow in brisk, short strokes. I finished up "All Along the Watchtower," nodded to the family from Peoria who had stopped to stare at me as if I were a roadside accident, laid down my Strat, and went over.

She launched into something lively and Irish sounding, her eyes closed, her head tilted thoughtfully to one side. I maintained my position as her entire audience until I was joined by a few skinny Parisian teenagers in black clothes, generating their own weather system of Gauloises smoke and attending to the music as if it were a philosophy lecture. When she finished, I tossed a few of my coins into her case to set an example, but it didn't make much of an impression on my associates, who moved quickly on down the line toward the guy who was walking on broken glass and eating fire. That bastard always had the crowd, and it had crossed my mind more than once to think up something a little more dangerous for myself, too. I didn't know how he did it. The glass was real, jagged and sharp — I'd checked it out.

"I know some bluegrass," I said to her, when it was just the two of us. "You want to play together? We'll double our income."

"You do? What do you know?"

I knew exactly four tunes, all of them learned to help out my college roommate with his senior thesis, "The Dave Katz Project." Katz had completed a music major without developing facility with any instrument, bravely working his way through the trumpet, the piano, and the upright bass, before finally settling on the banjo.

"'Sally Goodin'?" I said. "'Rocky Top?'" I didn't want to give her all four at once.

"'Sally Goodin'.'"

She came over to my spot and stood beside me as I slid my guitar back on. It was a midseventies model in a particularly ugly color called "Antigua," a kind of puke-and-cigarette-ash sunburst. I'd picked it up cheap from a guy I met in a record store who claimed he wanted to get rid of all his worldly possessions. It had a sawn-in-half baseball bat neck, and gouged into the back of the body was the legend "Satin Lives" — the work of some former owner with either poor spelling or a shiny wardrobe. I turned off my distortion and tried to get the cleanest, most mountain-pure sound I could. A few minutes earlier, I'd been blasting nuclear holocaust through that runt speaker. Now I wanted pine trees, moonshine whiskey, cold running streams. "There," I said, strumming a bright, open G.

"Wendy," she said, meeting my eyes briefly, without much interest. "I like to go fast." She stomped her foot three times.

Playing with The Dave Katz Project had always left me slightly depressed, since we never went fast — it was like sitting for the SATs. But Wendy took off like a bottle rocket. I thumped along, careful not to be too loud, trying to emphasize the bass notes and not let the pace drag. The Parisian teenagers came back. A small crowd began to gather.

The money rained in, copper, silver, even some notes. I asked her where she'd learned to play like that.

"Suzuki method. How about 'Cotton-eyed Joe'? It's just A-E-A."

When we'd done all we could to that one, a man with a bad hairpiece asked us if we wanted a job. He wore a suit and seemed reasonably believable when he said he could offer us 750 francs to play for the night, plus room and board. Wendy's French was slightly better than mine, and between the three of us we managed to clarify that the place we were going to was a sort of retreat for *les travailleurs* of the Renault automobile company. "They like very much the American music," he assured us. "John Denver."

In the van, I let my hand rest against Wendy's leg, which she didn't seem to notice. "I'm Phil," I said. She was staring out the window, so I did, too. The day had started out sunny and warm, but had been disintegrating since noon, and now it looked like rain. Jean, our host, drove us first to my hotel, where I grabbed my pack from the front desk — I'd checked out after breakfast and hadn't made any plan yet for tonight — then on to the youth hostel, where Wendy had her things. I'd learned she was from Baltimore, but that was about it. She seemed intent on not sharing much. I thought about what I might say to make myself seem interesting.

"How do you like France?"

"It's OK," she said. "I'm running out of money."

"We could make a killing together. We're eclectic."

"That's what that thing is? An eclectic guitar?" Her eyes were light green, almost feline. "I'm getting married in December."

"Good for you. Where is he, now?"

"Back home. Mad at me for being here."

"He should have come along. Does he play anything?"

"No. He doesn't really like music."

"And you want to marry him? Have you thought this thing through?"

She smiled, one side of her mouth going up higher than the other. "He voted for Reagan, too," she said. "It's sort of a problem."

It took about an hour to get where we were going, which was out in the country, and to the south. What we passed through to get there confirmed my suspicions that much of Europe was just an extension of the New Jersey Turnpike. Train tracks, concrete-bunker-style warehouses, power lines, freight yards, and ratty fields where they appeared to be raising weeds. Eventually we slid off into prettier territory, with farmhouses and trees. Then we were getting out in front of a big white house. Jean took us upstairs and showed us to our room.

We explored our quarters — twin beds with orange spreads on them, a sink in the room, a small bathroom off it with a toilet, tub (no bidet). I had found out a few things: she was twenty-four. She smoked Marlboros, lighting them with a World War II–vintage stainless steel Zippo. She had been traveling three weeks on an Inter-Rail Pass in France and Italy, busking infrequently, and with mixed success.

"They think we're together," she said, sitting on the edge of one bed.

I sat down beside her, but she got right up, went into the bathroom and brushed her teeth.

In the time we had before dinner, she showed me three more songs. I kept trying to rock-and-roll around underneath her traditional melodies, but she was having none of it. "Straight," she warned me. "Please, just keep the beat and hit the right chords."

Dinner was five courses of cafeteria-quality food, served to us at a table downstairs by a tiny blonde girl in a white jacket. I took it that this, the main house, was where Jean himself lived. Perhaps the girl was his daughter. It was meat, potatoes, green beans the color of army fatigues, cheese, fruit, and wine that tasted the way our family basement smelled, back before we'd had it fixed up and the carpeting installed. But it also wasn't pâté out of a can, and I paid attention, thinking I might live to tell someone about it sometime. *A five-course French meal!*

A path ran alongside the house and back to three one-story, concrete dormitories, as well as a central recreation building. They had a stage for us, with lights, even a small sound system. I gathered from a poster on the wall that we were the last-minute replacement for a ventriloquist who had canceled. Maybe Jean figured the broken-glass guy was too much of a fire hazard.

Our crowd was so drunk we could have been playing in different keys and they wouldn't have minded. There were about fifty of them, men and women, on foldout metal seats. Dress was casual. We played close to an hour.

Jean paid us in cash and told us when he'd take us back to the city in the morning. "I return you to the Beaubourg, yes?" he asked.

After he left us, Wendy grabbed my arm. "Come on," she said. "Let me show you something."

There was a phone booth in the courtyard. She took the receiver off and held her thumb over the button that turned the phone on and off. "You have to get it just right," she said. "OK. Who do you want to talk to?"

"No one."

"Don't you have a girlfriend or something?"

"No, not just now."

"Well, there must be someone you want to call. Give me a number." I told her my mother's. Keeping her thumb over the button, she used the forefinger of her other hand to tap sharply on it. "It's all in the rhythm," she said. She must have tapped fifty times. "Yes! Take it — it's ringing."

I huddled up next to her. The answering machine came on, and I left a cheery message — I was OK, I was making money, I'd write soon. Then I nodded and Wendy let up her thumb. "How does that work?"

"You can only do it with this kind of phone, but they have them all over. You keep the button out just far enough to get a dial tone, then tap the numbers. It takes some practice, but if you get the rhythm right, you can call anyplace for free."

She showed me, and for the next few minutes, I tried unsuccessfully to call my own number in Brooklyn. She told me to think in triplets — a nine was just a series of three threes — and that helped, but I eventually gave up. The whole business just reminded me that I had no one to talk to anyway. I'd illegally sublet my place to a guy named Clem who was a video technician down at CBS TV, in charge of making sure the right tapes ran between 2:00 a.m. and 6:00 a.m., when it was all just prerecorded programming. His bald head reminded me of a mushroom, and his dilated pupils and oddly timed way of speaking made me suspect he did a lot of hallucinogens, but he was the only person who had responded to my ad, and he'd paid cash in advance.

Back in the room, we smoked cigarettes by the window, the cool air bathing our hot faces, our bodies inches from each other. I told her about trying to be a musician in New York. I told her about how the house I'd grown up in, in New Jersey, was now for sale. My mom was moving in with Re-Pete, a bearded guy she'd met on the tennis courts, and my dad — Original Pete — had a new apartment.

"This friend of mine I knew from high school, Adam Gordon, comes in to this place where I'm waiting tables," I said. "He'd just spent a year playing his way around Europe. Paid for his whole trip. He gave me his map." I dug it out to show her. It was a Michelin one, with the good money towns circled in red, and it had been folded and refolded so often that it had the integrity of a laundered Kleenex.

"Been there," she said, studying it. "There, too. Want to go there, there, and there."

I thought about what else to tell her. My life seemed deeply uninteresting. This, right now, was probably the high point. My best friend might as well have been married — I never saw him anymore. I had one guy I hung out with back home, a Vietnam vet named Doggie John who washed dishes at the cafe. He and I would get stoned, go to Prospect Park, and throw the Frisbee to his Doberman pinscher, Ralph. Ralph had an inoperable brain tumor that made him blind in one eye, and as often as not, the Frisbee smacked him right in the side of the head.

"*Original Pete*," she said. "That's pretty funny."

"Not to him it isn't."

"No, I guess not."

"I'm glad we met," I said.

"I might go to law school. That's the other thing I'm thinking over. This is my thinking summer. Do you like martinis?"

"Not so much. I'm more of a shot-and-a-beer guy." I thought this might be the kind of thing a girl from Baltimore would like to hear.

"I love how they look. I love how the word sounds. And I've never had one. I'm not sure I want to. Then I'd have nothing to look forward to."

"There might be other things," I said.

"You understand that I couldn't possibly have sex with you?"

The moon was descending from a cloud, a big silver coin. I could feel the weather clearing. "What's he do? Your fiancé."

"Artist."

"Like a painter? A sculptor?"

"Yeah, like that."

"Does he at least have a name?"

"Tomislav."

"That sounds made up. Did he make it up?

"No, it's real. He's Serbian. From Yugoslavia."

"Ah," I said. "And votes Republican and hates music."

"He doesn't hate it. It's just not something he notices. It's funny when you think about it, because he's a gifted artist."

I stared at my boot, the toe of which had begun to come apart from the sole, and thought about how much I hated the word *gifted*.

"What?"

"Nothing."

"You can tell me." She reached out and touched my knee. "We ought to get to know each other."

"I'm not looking for sympathy."

"No one said you were."

"So, forget it."

"Forget what?"

"I'm not going to say."

"Sure you are." She exhaled through the screen. "Otherwise, I'm going to tickle you."

There was a bulge in the plaster where it had been resealed and painted over. The scar ran diagonally from the ceiling to the bottom of the window. "I have a tumor on the brain," I said, and then added, "inoperable."

"Are you serious? You're joking, aren't you?"

An uptown bus of a moment passed by, but I didn't get on. "You're right," I said. "I'm joking."

"Oh, my God." She took my hand. "You *aren't* joking. I knew a girl that happened to, back home, but they were able to operate. She was okay after the surgery. No hair, though." She touched mine, which hadn't been cut in a while, and was looking fairly wild. I hadn't shaved in a week. In general, I was pleased with how disreputable I looked. "Does it hurt?"

"Not usually. I feel like it's focused me, though."

"I'll bet."

"Sometimes I have visions. Brief ones."

"I get migraines, and right before, everything takes on an aura. Is it like that, or do you actually see things?"

"More like that."

"Brains are weird."

"Yes," I agreed. "They are."

"I'm really sorry about your head." She stood up, pushed her hair back behind her ears. "I'm going to take a bath."

"Knock yourself out." This was something Katz and I used to say.

She proceeded to take off all her clothes, right in front of me, then went into the bathroom and closed the door. I listened to the water as it fell into the tub, watched the light on my little amp in the corner where I'd plugged it in to recharge.

I'm ashamed to say that what followed was not a period of regret, or self-loathing, or anything like that — I found the role of dying musician fit me well. I almost began to believe it myself. Life took on a heightened quality — individual moments seemed artificially lit and oversaturated with color, like in a fifties musical. Occasionally I caught my own reflection in something — a bus window, the side-view mirror of a parked car — and noticed with satisfaction how nobly I seemed to be bearing up.

After Jean dropped us back in Paris, we went straight to the train station and headed to Switzerland, where the really good money towns were. Since what you earn as a street musician is the change in folks' pockets, you want to situate yourself in a country where the pocket change means something. Also, the Swiss are so orderly, so painfully aware of anything remotely out of place in their little windup towns, that they tend to throw money at you out of a kind of civic duty; they think if they pay enough, you'll go away. On a busy street in Bern, our first stop, we made nearly two hundred francs, and no one watched us for more than thirty seconds at a time.

We camped. Most towns had campgrounds on their outskirts, with reasonable facilities, a laundry room, perhaps even a Ping-Pong table or a bar. Wendy had a small tent, and every night, after a few hours of partying and maybe practicing a new song, we'd lay out our sleeping bags. I'd watch her kick out of her jeans, roll them up into a ball, then slide in. I grew to know her smell, which reminded me of sourdough bread. I learned the rhythm of her breathing when she slept, deep and even and a bit like surf. Occasionally, I'd make some kind of gesture — rub her shoulders, maybe, or try to nibble her ear — but although she'd let it go on for a minute or two, eventually she'd always push me away. When a campground had the right kind of phone, I'd practice my technique, calling the number of this nurse I'd gone out with one time, Rita, but with no luck. Foreign voices spoke to me, and I'd quickly hang up. I had no plan for what to do if I ever did get through, if Rita ever did answer. I knew she'd remember me. She was nice enough, older, maybe thirty, and had a kid. We'd eaten Chinese food at a place in the neighborhood. We'd just had nothing to say. Our waitress had taken our order, then disappeared for a long time. We'd heard shouting from the kitchen. We were the only people in the place. Finally, after another twenty minutes, during which she told me all about that evening's episode of *Wheel of Fortune*, the cook had come out to retake our order, very apologetically. He had almost no English at all, and we'd pointed to the items of the menu. For some reason, I still had Rita's number in my pocket.

A week passed, then another. We went up to Amsterdam, where I'd started my trip. The tall ships were coming, which meant crowds, which meant money. Money was the thing that kept us together, the subject of most of our conversations, the closest thing we had to a direction or goal. We stayed with Wild Bill, who ran a flophouse-style hostel, with strictly enforced house rules about being out of the house between 9:00 a.m. and 4:30 p.m., and required attendance at an afternoon tea at 5:00 p.m. He was Dutch, but long ago he had lived for a while in New York. Underneath his bossiness and generally irritable veneer, I suspected he was actually a nice guy. "Hey, look who it is," he said, when we showed up on his doorstep. "The Voodoo Child."

He gave us a room all to ourselves. It was tiny — there was barely space to stand up, but it had an actual bed in it, and even a tiny dresser. "Weren't you embarrassed?" she asked. "Going around pretending to be Hendrix?"

"It was like being in a tribute band," I said. "Just without the band. One of the few things I do well is imitating Jimi. I've been working on it since I was twelve. In high school, I was a god."

"You are *so* much better off with me." She broke off a piece of a Toblerone and popped it in her mouth, offered me the rest. "Listen, the Gnats are planning a big jam tomorrow night. They asked us to play." The Cashville Gnats were a bluegrass quartet made up of two Americans, upright bass and guitar, and a star banjo player named Jens, who was German and all of about sixteen. They had a mandolinist, too; I didn't know where he was from. We'd seen them in Bern and also Zurich — they always seemed to be leaving a town when we got there, or vice versa. It figured they'd come for the tall ships.

"How do you know?"

"I ran into Matt, the bass player, at the train station."

"You did?"

"When I went to get French fries. He was getting some, too."

"How come I didn't see him?"

"I don't know. Because you're oblivious? Anyway, I told him we'd come play."

"I don't want to play with them. We won't make any money."

"Maybe not, but it will be fun. Don't be a baby. Now, let's go see if we can find something to eat."

"Matt? How do you even know his name?"

"He told me. What's your problem?"

We played all the next morning down by the harbor. Two teenage girls had a stand selling soft ice cream cones, and around noon they brought us over a couple. The tall ships were due in the following morning, and the city was filling up with tourists. According to a headline I'd seen outside a newsstand, Iraq had just attacked

Iran, but both these places seemed so remote to me as to almost be fictional. My jeans pockets were stuffed to bursting with guilders, so heavy I'd had to crank my belt another notch to keep my pants up.

A young couple was making out on a bench, really going at it. Wendy took an extra-long lick at her ice cream, then cleared chocolate from the corner of her mouth with the end of her finger. "I should call Tomislav," she said.

"Why haven't you?" I'd been wondering this for a while. I'd even begun hopefully to entertain the idea that there might not *be* a Tomislav.

"That wasn't our deal. Our deal was time apart. You aren't apart if you keep checking in."

I crunched the rest of my cone, swallowed. "I'm going to have to leave," I said. "We're going to have to split up."

She licked again and thought some more. A group of big, black birds pecked at the cobblestones a few yards away. "You mean it?"

"I have to live life to its fullest. Carpe diem."

"Don't T-shirt philosophy me. Speaking of time, yours is improving."

"I didn't know anything was wrong with it."

"You drag a little. More than a little, actually. But you are getting better."

"Well, that's nice." I checked my watch. "We don't want to be late for tea. Bill will toss us out on our asses."

"What?" she said.

"Nothing."

"I told Matt we'd be there."

"I might hit Greece," I said. "Go lie on a beach someplace and eat grape leaves."

She was studying me. "All right."

"All right, what?"

"You know. Maybe the normal rules don't apply to us."

One of the crows took a vicious swipe at another. Then the lot of them took off over a warehouse like a gust of sooty wind.

In theory the things you want most, the things you've waited longest for, ought to be the sweetest, but everyone knows this isn't always true. The apples reddening so attractively on the tree turn out to be mushy or tasteless; the fantasized-about, dreamed-of career turns out to be just another desk in a cubicle in an office with bad air. The dope so delicately traced with red fibers turns out to give you a massive headache, the big game is a blowout, the expensive shoes just make your feet hurt.

I thought about getting a hotel or something, but we didn't have so much saved that we could afford to blow a lot of guilders. Plus, that would have made it a big deal, and the idea was that it was not. People assumed we were a couple anyway—certainly Bill did. To go check into some fancy place would have upped the stakes too much. This was casual. We just needed each other, and the bottle of Côtes du Rhône we picked up on the way back.

We'd had tea; we'd had dinner. There was still some pastel light coming through the tiny window by the bed. It all went reasonably well. She told me she'd remember me. "How?" I said. I was happy the way I was happy once on Halloween, when I'd gone out twice, in different costumes, spread out double the candy I deserved on the floor of my room and started to divide it taxonomically: Snickers and Baby Ruths, 3 Musketeers, Hershey's, right on down to the lowly boxed raisins and worthless candy corn. But she never answered. After a while, I realized she'd fallen asleep.

The next day we went out and made some money in the late morning, but then she wanted to rest, and I went for a long walk around the city. I was furious with myself, because I was pretty sure I was in love. I wanted more nights like last night. I thought about ways of fixing things. Did tumors ever just go away by themselves? I tried to imagine how that might happen. It wasn't something you just coughed up like a hairball. Perhaps I could be the recipient of miraculous news from the States. *It was a mistake. We mixed your X-rays up with someone else's! All is forgiven!*

I didn't want to play with the Gnats, and I was reasonably sure they didn't want me to play with them, either. One guitar is plenty for bluegrass. Plus, Wendy was right about my time — I couldn't even get the phone trick right. What they needed was a fiddle. I'd seen them watching us back in Zurich, enemy faces among the tourists, appraising, scouting our little Division III team for its pro-quality running back.

At 7:30 p.m., we all met down by the docks. Wendy had put on a sleeveless black top that showed off her figure, and she had a purple scarf that fluttered in the evening breeze. The ships had arrived, a leafless forest of masts and rigging. I remembered a book my father had bought for me when I was twelve, called simply *Pirates*. I searched the decks of these enormous vessels for men in breeches and blousy shirts. "They were ruthless," he'd told me. "They took what they wanted. They made up their own rules."

The air held the mingled harbor scents of fish and diesel exhaust and open ocean. I looked at her, I looked at the gathering Gnats, and then it hit me — the fix was already in. She hadn't just run in to the bass player — she'd made a deal with him. It was why she'd finally agreed to sleep with me — out of guilt. When we started up, I stood on the far side of the action, watching and listening as the five of them burned their way through some very professional-sounding stuff. I'd learned a lot from Wendy over the past weeks. We did "Uncle Pen," and "Salt Creek," and "Way Downtown." They had other, more complicated material up their sleeves, too, including "Take Five," and a banjo version of "Flight of the Bumblebee." I sat those out, resentment growing in me. When it came my turn to solo on "Foggy Mountain Breakdown," I stomped on the fuzz pedal, and started playing Jimi's solo from the Woodstock version of "Fire." A couple of people cheered.

In a jam, it's customary to take two choruses, then shut up and let the next guy go. Maybe if you're all having a good time, you go around again. But I wouldn't stop. I did all my tricks: between the legs, behind the back, playing with my teeth (you don't actually get your teeth on the strings, but it looks that way). From "Fire," I segued into "The Star-Spangled Banner." Mostly, I was just making noise. There were maybe a hundred people watching, hundreds more moving past along the waterfront behind them, enjoying the cool evening, happy to be out and about where people were alive and mingling, and where there were tall ships.

By the time I was done the Strat was out of tune and I was sweating profusely. I stepped back and avoided Dennis's icy stare. Wendy was clearly mortified, but I didn't care. I unstomped my pedal and tried to strum along, but it sounded so bad that I just turned down the volume and stood there, watching as Jens took center stage again, sending busy, silvery ladders of notes up into the night sky.

"You are a jerk," she told me, when we took a break.

"I knew what was going on as soon as I saw that scarf."

"You're crazy."

"It's like a signal or something."

"Was that one of your visions? It's a *scarf*. I thought it would look nice."

Jens was signing autographs. The other Gnats were popping open bottles of Grolsch, with those cute little porcelain stoppers.

"I'm not dying," I said. She just stared at me. "The cancer thing is a dog I know, Ralph. I just borrowed it." The perspiration at my collar was getting chilly with the breeze coming in off the water. "So, I'm a jerk. Proven. It was a stupid lie, but I didn't think it mattered because we'd never see each other again anyway, and now I see that it does matter and I can't do anything about it." I hoisted my gig bag over my shoulder and picked up the amp. "I'm going back to Bill's," I said. "Have fun with your new friends." After a few steps, I stopped and turned. "Aren't you going to say anything?"

"Like what? That I'm disappointed?"

"You didn't say I was wrong."

"Maybe I knew all along," she said. "Did you ever think of that?"

She came in very late that night, smelling of beer, climbed into bed, and turned her back to me. I listened to her sleep and thought this must be what a marriage feels like after it's gone past the point of repair.

In the morning, Bill's houseboy brought us coffee and a cinnamon muffin as he always did. "They're invited to three festivals in the States next summer," said Wendy, brushing crumbs off her napkin and writing her address and phone number down for me. "I'm playing with them tomorrow at the Leidseplein. Then, in a week, I'm going home."

I did the same for her with mine. It seemed we were done talking about it, which was probably best anyway. "Just remember," I pointed out, "now you're looking at a five-way split."

I went to Germany. For eight humid days, I traveled and busked with a harp player I met in Heidelberg, a short Austrian named Ernst, but he smelled bad and sang even worse, and one night I woke up in the park where we were sleeping to find him attempting to make off with Satin Lives. I tackled him, but he surprised me with a head-butt, grabbed the guitar and ran off into the night. I figured it was a sign.

The number Wendy had given me turned out to be for a bar at a driving range outside of Bel Air, Maryland. "Nineteenth Hole," the guy said, when I called from the Brussels airport. Our connection had a bad echo. Three days since my fight with Ernst and my head still hurt. I couldn't believe I'd finally gotten the phone trick to work.

I asked anyway.

"Windy?" he shouted. "I don't know — I'm inside. They were talking rain for later on. You sound long distance. Are you long distance?"

I let my thumb up and broke the connection. I was across from the duty-free shop, the window of which displayed a new brand of vodka, cobalt-blue bottles lined up at attention and shimmering in the terminal light. About thirty yards further along toward the gates, in a waiting area, a skinny guy with dreadlocks and a bad complexion was juggling beanbags. I went over and watched him for a while. He was good with three and with four, but with five he kept dropping bags. Before I left, I unloaded the rest of my change into his hat.

SANTORINI

The Australian girl and Harrison were standing about two feet apart in the center of the hotel pool, discussing the respective merits of the American and Australian versions of MTV. Rivulets of water ran down the pronounced *V* of Harrison's chest, the result of his last submersion. Every now and then, he dunked himself down into the water, then popped back up and shook his long hair like a dog. The girl was blonde, generically pretty, with a ponytail, on vacation with her family, and in the noon sun her white bikini top was blindingly bright — a special effect above her prominent ribcage and below her strong swimmer's shoulders.

Flo poked Laura's foot.

"I see," said Laura, who had been imagining the girl in a sunny freefall over the cliff edge, two hundred yards down to the shimmering Aegean.

"It's so *cute.*"

The girl got out of the pool and dried herself with a towel, wrapped a see-through white skirt around her waist, and climbed up the steep whitewashed steps that led to the pool area. Above, the apartments of Sunshine Villas spilled down off the rim of the caldera, clinging to the steep sides. A few moments later, Harrison came over and settled himself into a chair next to his mother's. Laura watched the moisture on his tanned skin as it evaporated. She thought she could feel him counting, trying to decide how long was long enough not to seem obvious. Then he reached over and tapped Flo's shoulder.

"I'm going for a walk."

"Pick up a bottle of water for the room, would you, honey?"

He stood, retrieved the novel he'd been reading from the arm of his chair and closed it, then looked over at Laura. "Going for a walk."

"Of course you are," she said.

He hesitated, then turned and headed up the steps.

"I didn't know bodies like that existed in the real world," Flo said. "I was always told they had something to do with airbrushes."

"She's got a nice butt, I'll give her that. Did you hear her accent? Every sentence ends in a question mark."

"I heard her say something about a 'life of bread.' What do you suppose that is?"

"Not *life*. *Loaf*. A *loaf* of bread. I think she might have been talking about lunch."

Flo burst out laughing. "I was lying here thinking she must work in a bakery. I'm so dumb. Do you think he's meeting her?"

"What do you think?"

"She seems a little old. But you have to admire him for trying. 'A life of bread.' Wow. What would that even be?"

"Sounds kind of nice to me," Laura said. "Warm. Comfy. You want to split a salad? Since it's just us girls?"

Flo sat up and retied her yellow bikini top around her neck. She looked good, Laura thought, in spite of her bouts of sadness. They both did. At home, Laura ran five miles every other day, went to the gym the days in between. In Athens, the desk clerk at their hotel had assumed they were part of the college tour.

"Here's to a life of bread," Flo said, when their salad came. They'd ordered a cold bottle of the local retsina, too, and each held a glass.

Laura's shoulders were starting to ache from the sun. She hated how she felt right now. She thought about the Australian girl's breasts. They weren't her fault — she was a teenager. She was supposed to look like that. Laura checked her watch.

"Don't worry," said Flo cheerfully. "Harry's a big boy. He can take care of himself." She speared an olive with her fork and popped it in her mouth.

On their third night in Athens, Harrison had come up to the hotel's rooftop garden where Laura was drinking bourbon and staring out at the Acropolis. She was forty, the veteran of long-term relationships with three perfectly decent men, as well as shorter ones with a couple of jerks. The last long one — a guy named Franz — had ended two weeks before, when he'd announced he was in love with his ex-wife, and tonight a sense of squandered time had crept inside her and made her weepy. She knew it would go away — it always did — but since she'd allowed it to come in, she didn't mind serving it a few drinks. When Harrison sat down next to her in the dark, she didn't even realize who it was at first.

"The Turks ruined the view," he said. "But the lights are nice."

"What do you know about Turks?" she asked.

"They wear those funny little hats. Sidney Greenstreet in *Casablanca*."

Flo had gone to bed two hours earlier. Unripe grapes hung down from the trellis above their heads. Harrison put a hand on her arm, then took it away. From the pocket of his cargo shorts he produced a plastic bottle of Old Crow and poured some carefully into his glass, then gestured toward hers. She pushed the glass forward.

"I'm allowed to drink, so long as I don't do anything stupid," he said.

"Define *stupid*."

"Puking your guts out and going to the hospital, I suppose. Stealing. Getting arrested, for whatever. Doing drugs, or getting caught doing drugs. My dad's a big common sense man. 'Just use your common sense,' he likes to say."

"How is your dad?"

"OK. He's taken up calligraphy. *Tensho, reisho, kaisho, gyosho,* and *sosho.* Those are your five major styles."

They sat in silence for a while, then he put his hand on hers. Their table was in the farthest corner of the garden. At the opposite end, some kids from the college program were having beers. She thought there was probably some obvious course of action she was supposed to take here, some profoundly adult way of defusing the situation.

"I've had a big crush on you since I was five," he said.

"That's ridiculous. You know that, right?"

"I used to look through my mom's photo albums with her. I thought you were what a Beatles song would look like if it could walk around."

"And that doesn't even make sense," she said.

He stroked her arm and she closed her eyes. This went on for quite a while. When she opened them, his face was next to hers, huge, like something projected on a drive-in movie screen. When he kissed her, she felt nerve endings snapping to attention as far down as her toes. She looked around, afraid of making a scene.

"I've got cheese in my room," she said. "Crackers, too."

At 5:30, he went into the bathroom and washed himself with the handheld shower, then toweled off, waved, and slipped back up to his mother's room. His story, if she asked, was that he'd gone over to one of the twenty-four-hour tavernas at the nearby meat market to have a bowl of *patsas* — a tripe soup he'd read about in their guidebook.

Alone, Laura lay staring up at the ceiling. She imagined herself two years from now flying back East, renting a car, and driving up to some New England college, getting a room at the nearest Holiday Inn so that she could spend time with him between classes. She planned her wardrobe: white Capri pants, oversized Gucci sunglasses, maybe a big platinum wig. She was a fool, an idiot, a cliché, probably in need of psychological help. And yet she felt as giddy and bad as she had back in tenth grade, when Malcolm Muri had introduced her to bong hits, and she'd gone to seventh period English and pretended her pencil was a rocket ship.

Around two, Flo disappeared, then came back and announced she'd rented them wheels.

"Who's driving?" asked Laura. She had put the umbrella up, and had been staring at the same page of her book for nearly an hour. "Not you?"

"Peter and I had one in Bermuda. They're easy. I want to go up to that town at the top of the island. Come on, I got you a helmet and everything."

"What about Harrison?"

"He's fine. We'll leave him a note."

They went upstairs and changed into jeans. The bike was parked out in the road, and Laura was impressed with how expertly Flo maneuvered it around to her. She got on behind and put her arms around Flo's waist.

"Don't be scared," said Flo.

"Don't scare me."

After a few minutes, when it became apparent that they weren't going over the edge of any cliffs, she began to relax. Flo drove carefully, slowing for the extreme, tight turns. There were views down to the ocean, and strange volcanic rock formations. The wind flew in their faces and whistled inside their helmets. When they arrived in Oia, they walked through its narrow streets, then found a taverna with a view and ordered wine and bread. Laura felt slightly dizzy.

Flo's brown hair was broken up in places by gray streaks, but that just made her prettier. Her eyes were a luminous gray-green. Laura had always envied her looks. "Steve Zablatnik," she said. "From Cleveland, Ohio."

"Who?"

"Your guy, from Pelekas."

"Why would you bring him up?" Twenty years earlier, they'd camped for five days on a Corfu beach that was a popular destination for foreigners, many of whom sunbathed in the nude. Laura remembered Steve. He'd had long hair, worn a big straw hat with a colorful band around it, sold hashish or something.

"Can I tell you something?" Flo looked away, out toward where the sun hung over the top of a ruined Venetian fortification.

"You can tell me anything. You know that."

"It's just this thing I've had all these years, and it's always bothered me."

"About Steve Zablatnik?"

"Yeah."

"Wait — are you saying what I think you're saying?"

Flo's face turned a blotchy crimson. Laura reached out for her hand. "It's okay. I barely remember his name. That was a lifetime ago. I'm just amazed."

"I was jealous because there you were having a hot summer romance, the kind people dream of having, and then he started coming on to me one night and we just sort of sneaked off. I don't even think you noticed we were gone."

"It's nothing."

"It's not. It's horrible. I worry sometimes about myself, that I could have done something like that. It's not me."

"Listen," said Laura, "forget it. Don't give it another thought."

"But maybe Steve Zablatnik was the guy you were destined to fall in love with and marry, and I got in the way."

"Could you be a little more dramatic, please? He isn't even a blip on my radar screen. I'm fine about it. He's probably in jail, or bald."

"Still, it would mean a lot if you'd say you forgive me."

Laura picked at a rough nail on her index finger. Since her divorce, Flo had been highly emotional, sometimes calling Laura at 3:00 a.m. for reassurance that she was, indeed, a good person. Laura hadn't said anything about Franz, just hinted that they were having problems, hints Flo never addressed. "There's nothing to forgive. I barely remember his face."

"Maybe you could say it anyway?"

"You're forgiven. There, feel better?" She handed her a napkin. "Go on and blow your nose. That always helps. I don't know why, but it does."

Harrison rejoined them for dinner at a taverna in town. He had on a new dark brown T-shirt with a dolphin on it, but didn't have anything to say about his afternoon. Laura drank too much during the meal, and insisted that they all stick around and listen to the bouzouki musicians. She could feel herself getting overly loud and cheerful. They had four more days here. Then it was back to Athens for another day before returning to the states. To what? Last month she'd taken an apartment at a development on the edge of Colorado Springs called Falcon Landing. Franz had helped her move, then made his announcement. She had money — that wasn't a problem. She just didn't know where she was supposed to *be*. On the second night in her new place, coyotes had eaten her cat.

The change in Harrison, the way he was avoiding her eyes and seemed so impatient to get back to the hotel, made her angry. Worse, it made her feel stupid.

"*Karpoozi*," she told the waiter, "and ouzo all around." She had learned a few Greek words, determined not to feel like a complete moron this time around, surrounded by sounds she could not interpret and signs she couldn't read. *Mele. Nero. Ne, oki. Kalimera, kalinikta.* In their hotel in Athens, she'd watched the better part of a dubbed *Sesame Street*, an episode brought to her by the number *decapende*, which she was pleased to have figured out meant *fifteen*.

When the melon came, she picked up a slice and bit into it open mouthed, letting the juice wander down the sides of her mouth before she picked up her napkin. The waiter returned with three half glasses of liquor.

"You're going to corrupt him," said Flo. "Imagine if either of our parents had come along with us last time."

"Let's not."

Harrison sipped his drink and made a face. "You were a couple of wild women back then, huh?"

"The amazing thing, Harrison," said Laura, "is that when I look at your mother, she doesn't seem any different."

"I'm a castoff. A used-up tube of toothpaste," said Flo.

Harrison checked his watch.

"No one here is a tube of anything," said Laura. "Come on."

"You're right. I am so lucky," said Flo, holding her hands out. "I have the best son anyone could ask for, and the best friend, too."

In the morning, Harrison was only interested in staying around the hotel. "You guys take the bike to the beach," he said. "You don't need me getting in the way."

"What are you going to do?" Laura asked. She'd put on shorts and a tight T-shirt that read "Cycladic Museum."

"Chill by the pool, finish my book. See if any of the women take off their tops."

"We could rent a second bike," said Flo. "Just for you. My license, you get to drive. Just make sure you don't get stopped by the cops."

"It's OK," he said. "I'm fine."

"You must be fine to turn down an offer like that," said Flo. "Take the boy to Greece and he discovers Australia."

Harrison blushed.

"It's OK, honey. We're rooting for you." She put on her sunglasses and opened the door onto their balcony. White light exploded into the room. "I'm going to pick up some things at the market for lunch."

Alone, Laura and Harrison stared at each other. "Well?" she said, finally.

"Know what this country needs? A really good hamburger."

"Don't change the subject."

"I'm sure you guys will have a fun day."

"Your attention span is that short? Some blonde bunny shows up and that's it?"

"Um," said Harrison.

"Because mine isn't."

He put his arms around her. She moved against his wiry body, but after a bit, he pushed away. "It's a little too weird," he said.

She touched his hair. "Of course," she said. "You're right. But I'd like to point out that you started this."

"I think I might be in love."

"What happened? Tell me what happened. Did you hold hands? Kiss? Did you make love? Please don't tell me you made love."

He lowered his eyes for a moment. "The first two."

"This isn't fair," she said. "You don't get to reject me, OK? We're on vacation, and vacation time is different. It's like eating standing up in front of the refrigerator — it doesn't really count. You should trust me on this. I know a few things. And I'm quite sure you are not in love."

"How would you know?" He looked at her in a way she'd seen before in men. Already, he was growing into the hardness, the certainty. He had the same square jaw as his father, and his blue eyes.

"You don't have a clue what love is."

"And you do?"

"I know it isn't like some cartoon hammer that materializes out of nowhere and bonks you on the head."

"What is it like, then?"

She pushed at him with the flat of her hand in a way that seemed lame to her — a girly punch. "More like a virus that grows inside of you, slowly, until it has taken over all your vital organs. Until you are nothing but a host."

At the beach, they swam, sunbathed, swam some more. With her goggles on it seemed to Laura that she was flying — she'd had dreams like this — and that the strange, bubbled-rock ocean floor she could see sloping sharply beneath her was actually miles away. Striped fish wandered past her without interest. Face down and floating, she could just bob around in the waves and watch, search for signs of the upcoming eruption. She could also keep her mind off any thoughts of what might be going on back at the hotel.

"You told me something," she said, after they'd eaten the bread, Swiss cheese, and ham Flo had brought along for them in her daypack, "so now I'm going to tell you something."

Flo handed her half a peach, dripping juice.

"Harrison and I have had sort of a thing."

"What do you mean 'a thing'?"

"You know. Like a romantic thing."

Flo took a bite of peach, chewed and swallowed. "What?"

"You, me, Steve Zablatnik." Having come this far, she was incapable of putting the situation into a coherent sentence. "Like on Corfu. Sneaking off."

"You've been sneaking off with Harrison?"

"Listen, I am so, so sorry."

Flo looked at her in disbelief. "Why are you telling me this? Why would you want to hurt me like this?"

"I don't want to hurt you. I love you."

"That's some way of showing it. My son? How could you do that? What kind of person are you?"

"Dumb. Just stupid. Miserable, right now. I don't know what happened. It was sort of an accident. It's over, of course. I know right now you can't, but I hope you'll find a way to forgive me eventually."

Flo took the remaining portion of her peach and threw it into Laura's face. It glanced off the side of her cheek and landed in the sand. "*I* made this happen," she said. "By bringing up Steve Zablatnik."

"You didn't."

"I know I didn't, but I feel that way. And if I hadn't said anything, then you probably wouldn't have either, and then I wouldn't have to know what a sick, crummy person you really are. I'd still have a friend I loved and trusted."

"You do. Really, you do."

"No," she said, her voice breaking. She began to gather her things. "I don't. I don't have anything. Have you got money?"

"I think so."

"Good. Because you're going to have to take the bus back. I won't be responsible for driving us both, and I don't think I want you that close to me."

"All right," said Laura.

In less than a minute, Flo was back, looking for the keys she'd forgotten. She bent down, momentarily blocking the sun.

"Franz dumped me," Laura said.

"What?" said Flo. "Who?"

"Nothing." She poked her finger into the hot sand. "Forget it."

Laura looked out the bus window and saw the green Peugeot motorbike bent and on its side like a stepped-on insect. The small truck it had collided with had pulled over a few yards past the intersection. A dark, wet patch on the road might have been blood, but could just as easily have been oil or gas. Then they were past the scene, the bus rattling and gaining speed. She gripped the railing in front of her and tried not to think at all.

Harrison met her at the door to their suite. "She doesn't want to see you," he said. "She wants you to find another place to stay. She wishes you'd go home."

"What happened?"

"Wipe out. She hit a truck, or one hit her — I don't know. She's all scraped up, but nothing's broken. She won't go to the hospital. Kelly took a look at her. She's a nurse."

"Well, that's convenient."

"I gotta go see the guy at the bike place." He pushed past her out the door, then turned around, this time looking right at her, his expression full of simple outrage. "You told her," he said.

"I did."

"Why?"

She had no answer for this. "Kelly," she said, feeling the sound of it on her tongue. It was a volleyball name, a parents-have-money, not-too-bright-but-very-nice-and-cheery name. You could have kids with a Kelly, drive them to private school in your new minivan, kicking up dust behind your tires as you crossed the outback, dodging kangaroos.

Laura was able to get another room, a studio at the very top of the steps to which the desk clerk had her things moved, but there was no quick way off the island. She couldn't change her plane ticket back to Athens, and while there were ferries, none had cabins available, and she didn't want to spend an entire night sitting on deck.

At breakfast, Harrison hurried past her without a word, clutching his bowl of granola. Her new room had been dug right into the side of the cliff and felt like a cave. She spent as much of the day as she could there, some of it sitting on the balcony in the sun, the rest sprawled on her double bed with the air-conditioning running. There was no television, just a little speaker with a knob by the bed that had crackly preprogrammed music. In the afternoon, she heard Harrison laughing with the Australian girl as they passed up the steps and out the gate to the road.

She wrote a card to Franz, one she'd picked out for him in Syntagma Square, with a picture of a kouros on it that she thought he might like. *An idealized sculpture of a young man.* When she read over what she'd written, she was embarrassed at how thin it sounded, how falsely cheerful, and she tore it into pieces. Pretending at being friends after breaking up was just a big lie, a way of prolonging the pain. At least this time, maybe she was smart enough to believe in what had happened and not start telling herself other stories. Of course he still loved his ex-wife. Of course. She wrote another card to her mother in New York, telling her about all the stray cats there were in Greece.

At sunset, she considered going down to Flo's room with a bottle of retsina, but then thought better of it and instead drank by herself, staring out over the water. Time would have to pass, that was all. She tried to decide which Beatles song she'd be, if she were one. "Eight Days a Week," if she had her choice, but "Eleanor Rigby" seemed more likely. Shortly after dark, she went to bed and dreamed that warm, fragrant loaves of bread were flying slowly past her like fat birds, just out of reach.

She was awakened by a tapping at the door. "What?" she said. "Who is it?"

"Me," said Harrison.

She got up and slipped on a big denim shirt, buttoning it on her way to the door, which she unlocked and opened.

"Please?" he said. "Can I come in?"

"How is she?"

"Doing better. She's got a nasty bruise on her right thigh. The bike's trash, though. I thought the rental guy was going to cry."

"Where's what's-her-name?"

"We went to a club to dance, and the next thing I know, she's with some other guy. I hung around a little while longer, but I felt stupid."

"Sucks to be ditched, huh?"

He said nothing.

"I was asleep," said Laura. "And now I'm going back."

"You look beautiful."

"Oh, cut the crap. You just want to feel better about yourself, and you think sex with me might do the trick."

He sat on the edge of her bed and picked a bag of cashews up off the night table, took one out and ate it. When he looked up at her again, she saw that his eyes were shiny.

"I've got nothing for you," she said. "You know what I said about eating in front of the refrigerator? I was lying. Vacations are as real as anything."

"Kelly told me all about Pelekas beach," he said. "Where you guys were? She's been there."

"No, she hasn't," said Laura. "Not to our beach. I know what it's like now— there's a road to it, and hotels. When we went, you had to climb down a steep, narrow path, through olive trees and brush. There was nothing, just a tiny taverna at either end where you could get an oily omelet." As she spoke other things came to her mind, the strange group of drunken Brits who had built themselves a complex of glass huts, decorated the outsides with animal skulls, and flown a Jolly Roger. The boy she'd made love with in a canvas tent, hearing the sounds of the ocean only yards away. "She's been someplace, I'm sure, but she hasn't been there. The place we went had pirates."

"She said she had," said Harrison. He wore a black T-shirt, baggy shorts, and leather sandals inside which his big, knobby feet managed somehow still to be attractive. Last summer she had grown peppers in her garden, and he reminded her of how they'd looked before they were ready to be picked, pushing hard against the confines of their own skins.

"*Kalinikta*," said Laura.

After the door clicked shut behind him, she went back out on the balcony with some cheese and crackers and sat staring out over the ocean. Across the water, on the island of Thirasia, a few tiny lights burned. She wondered if someone over there was looking at her right now, seeing the sparkle of her own lights and envying the fine time she must be having. A cat hopped down from the wall behind her and rubbed up against her leg. It was a spindly, beaten-up thing, mostly white, and missing one eye. She put a bit of cheese on the ground, and it quickly gobbled this down. She broke off a bit more, and it ate that, too. She missed her own cat, Spiderman, who used to sleep atop the stereo. She'd only had him a year. As if materialized out of the air, there were two more, a black one and a tabby. "You hungry, too?" she said to them, tossing more cheese. Another tabby appeared, followed by a gray one, missing an ear. All the cats seemed veterans of multiple, vicious fights. "Here, guys," she said. They jumped for the morsels, and Laura began to feel less attracted to them — she wished they would go away. She could smell them. Three more hopped down from the wall, and now her balcony was alive with mewing, hungry cats. One of them took a nasty swipe at the beaten-up white one, and it cringed into a corner, an unreadable expression pinned to the wall by moonlight.

THE NAKED MAN

I hadn't always been *The Naked Man*. While his head was mine — dark curly hair, glasses, an earnest, somewhat baffled look on a middle-aged face with an almost blue beard line and what I like to think of as a dueling scar on the left cheek (I had a cyst removed there and the doctor botched the job) — the body belonged to my wife's former boyfriend, a man with the unlikely name of Garth, who taught earth science at a high school in Ohio. Garth had posed for other paintings, too, but this was the last, and the only one he'd done nude. To make him feel better about his slight paunch (he probably had ten pounds on me), she'd exaggerated his private parts, but she hadn't finished the painting when they split up. The face was still only blocked in, and for various reasons, she didn't feel right about having it be Garth's at all anymore. "What do you think?" she asked me. "You'll impress the world." And I have to admit, it did enter into my thinking when I agreed.

Tina had been accepted for a show at a nonprofit gallery in Virginia, and though we debated going, when the time came, we'd decided to make a trip out of it. It was probably our last as just the two of us, since our baby, Frick, which was what we were still calling him, was due in May, and it was already February. Now we were at this party at a house right out of the pages of *Architectural Digest*, planted in the middle of horse country, ten miles from town and at least a half mile from the country road we'd followed to get here. Earlier tonight had been the preopening opening, especially for benefactors and supporters. The gallery had used me, in a detail from the painting, for the postcard advertising the show. My head, Garth's body, this composite naked man standing on a country path holding a shopping bag full of groceries, staring out into space as if trying to remember some item he'd forgotten to purchase. So that the image would be acceptable to the post office, they'd designed a little sticker in the shape of a pair of red boxers to affix to each card. It was pretty cute. All night, people had been eyeing me, trying to remember where we'd met before. Then it would hit them. They'd look at me, they'd look at Tina, with her swollen belly. They'd look back at me and smile.

I rejoined Tina in the living room. I knew she was worried. "You ought to see the bathroom," I said, placing my wine carefully on the glass coffee table. "One whole wall is see-through." In fact, there wasn't a door in the house, other than the ones leading outside.

"Just imagine trying to sell this place," she said. We talked about real estate a lot. We were in a little over our heads in that respect, having bought a row house two years ago, at the top of the market. Our neighbor, an older guy who'd purchased the rental property next door back in the sixties for ten bucks and a carton of Lucky Strikes, was always looking at me like I was Ed McMahon, come to deliver him his Publishers Clearing House check. But I knew — it would be a long while before anything in the neighborhood sold for near what we'd paid. I could hear the value escaping from our walls like air hissing out of a leaky tire. I was upside down on the store, too, and in general, money was keeping me awake nights.

"You couldn't," I said. "It's too strange."

"Anyone who bought it would have to change who they were to accommodate the house."

I moved with her to the floor next to the enormous fireplace, which was not part of a wall, but away from it, with a black metal chimney that shot up a good twenty feet before meeting the steeply angled roof. All around us, the partiers were happily chattering away. The two other artists held court in the opposite corners, enjoying their celebrity. One was an older guy who taught at a prestigious college someplace and did small paintings that seemed to be scenes from a love affair — a messed-up bed, someone peering through Venetian blinds, a half-finished drink sweating on a desk next to a fan. Then there was this tall kid with hip eyeglasses and a ski hat whose six-foot canvases were staged images of his girlfriend and other people in his life in the aftermath of some violent event, sporting bruises, bloody lips, etc. He'd assured us earlier that no one had actually gotten hurt. It was all just theater.

"Anything?" I asked.

"Nope." It had been a few hours since she'd felt the baby. Tina's hair had grown long and thick over the past months, and was now well past her shoulders. Her full breasts pressed against the flower-print top she'd bought to wear for this trip. Back home, when she wasn't going in to teach at the college, she lived mostly in a pair of stripy pajama bottoms.

"Did you drink water?"

"I drank water. I lay down. I stood back up. I did the jerk. It's like he stepped out for a cigarette break."

"Heartburn?"

"No more than usual."

"I'm going to call the store," I said.

"Go ahead."

After a few rings, Hobey picked up. Between the noise of this party, and the one that seemed to be going on in Baltimore, it was hard to communicate. "You OK?" I shouted. A man across the room with a white suit and a pink tie turned to look at me and I smiled.

"Fine!" sang Hobey. I'd taken her on mostly because she was a wizard at changing guitar strings, and it turned out that this was a service I needed to provide the public on a regular basis. I'd bought a little mom-and-pop music store last year from a guy named Edelman, who was now someplace in Florida, supposedly, although I was having a hell of a time contacting him. It turned out that a lot of the stock I'd paid him for — much of it dusty and dating back to at least the eighties — was in fact still the property of various manufacturers who had given up on Edelman years ago, but now, smelling fresh blood in the water, were circling again, sending me letters suggesting litigation, boycott, and ruin. I did most of my business in lessons, strings, and picks. But I got to be around guitars all day, which was something I'd always thought I'd like, and sometimes I imagined little Frick in there with me, crawling around in the dust balls, knocking over music stands.

"You practicing?" I'd told her Hobey and the Lesbians could rehearse in the shop, so long as they kept it down and quit by eleven.

"Yeah!" she shouted. "How's the show?"

I poked Tina, who was sniffing the cookie I'd brought her. "How's the show?"

"So far, so good."

"Good!" I said. This call was beginning to feel pointless. I imagined the scene back there. Hobey and her girlfriend the bass player, her buddies Jason and Jeremy on drums and keys, working their way through a case of National Bohemian. Hobey fully admitted to needing more lesbians in Hobey and the Lesbians, but Jason and Jeremy were filling in for now, and didn't seem fazed by their temporary status. I envied all of them. They were driven by energy and optimism about the future. They had an actual gig upcoming in the spring, at a women's collective in Greektown.

"And Frick?" she shouted.

"Sound asleep," I said.

"I wish you wouldn't talk to her about us," said Tina, when I hung up. "It feels like bad luck."

The financial advice guy was winding down the speech he was giving to some horsey-set lady who actually had on riding boots, and I could tell he had his eyes on us for next. I'd never been at a party where people wanted to be around me so much.

"I've got a buyer for *The Naked Man*," I told her. "She approached me in the bathroom. That Broccoli woman."

"This is her house."

"I know that."

"In the bathroom?"

"They have the bar set up in there. Don't ask me why."

"What did you tell her?"

"NFS. I think she might be related to those movie people, the ones who do all the Bond films."

"That's interesting," said Tina. She didn't like movies. Her paintings were narrative oils depicting imaginary adventures of Marco Polo: as a tourist at a provincial museum full of dusty, strange objects, or being welcomed by beautiful girls to a city that was in fact nothing but a painted set, behind which you could see the crumbling facades of the real buildings. The paintings were about perception and reality, about xenophobia, about appropriation. They took about 150 hours each, and were excruciatingly detailed — she was a big Fra Angelico fan. But the main thing about them was that they were not for sale. In the time we'd been together, she had yet to agree to sell a single one of them. She needed them all so she could try to get into a New York gallery. The irony of this did not escape either of us, although we didn't talk about it much. If she did get a fancy gallery to take her on, and they sold these pieces, it would be years before she'd have enough work for another show. With the kid, maybe longer. Of course, I loved her paintings, even the one with me in it (Marco Polo chooses to scramble off the path I'm walking along rather than confront me, even though the vegetation is all thorns and cacti and there are bees — it was one of her funnier scenes), loved having them hang on our walls when they weren't out at some show. But a commodity is a commodity, I kept telling her. If art is your business, you figure out a way to make it economically viable. You sell your work.

"Did you eat anything? They have a lot of good stuff. Not just those designer hot dogs. There's veggie lasagna."

"I'm not so hungry." She sniffed the cookie again.

"You're always hungry."

"Thank you. Am I supposed to be worried or not? Whatever you say, I'll try for that. But could you try to be consistent?"

"Absolutely," I said. "I'll be consistent."

"So which is it?"

"We're not worrying." I stroked her leg. "Everything's fine."

Maybe it really was the drugs. Back in high school, my friends and I always used to joke about the ridiculous things they wanted you to believe, that LSD would screw up your genes (not to mention make you turn into Art Linkletter's daughter and try flying off a roof). Your kids would come out with two heads, or bicycle wheels instead of feet. For whatever reason, I wasn't worried. I was certain that when I decided to have kids, despite my misspent youth, I'd be able to.

But we couldn't, Tina and I. We started trying right after the wedding. It was late for both of us — she was thirty-four, I was forty-three — but I still expected to knock the first pitch right into the stands. Instead, I struck out swinging. We tried different positions. We monitored her temperature, circled days on the calendar, went out for romantic meals followed by elaborate desserts. After a year, we went in for tests. The results were interesting.

Oligospermia. Astenozoospermia. Teratozoospermia. Low count, lousy swimmers, misshapen anyway. This, in spite of the fact that my college girlfriend had hit me up for three hundred dollars for an abortion, something I now considered to have been unlikely to have been related to me. Enter "Brad." "Brad" is what I called him, of course. Cryo-Logic, the company we eventually settled on, called him N311. For close to a month, Tina was glued to her computer every night, going through the profiles. Before we'd met, she'd done some computer dating, and she brought all her skills to bear on this new problem. Eye color, education, height, ancestry, religion. It was daunting.

"I sort of want a vegetarian," she said.

"I'm not a vegetarian," I pointed out. "Shouldn't you want someone like me?"

"Of course," she said. "Of course."

For more money, you could get more info. Some places allowed you to see adult photos of the guys, but I drew the line at that. I didn't want her hearing voice clips, either, although that was a possibility with an upgraded membership. What did they sound like? "Hello, my name is Brad. I like walking on the beach, sunsets, and old Billy Joel songs, from before he met Christy Brinkley. I hope you'll choose me."

And now, Brad had begot Frick, who had somehow managed to grab onto my wife's uterine wall and ontogenically recapitulate phylogeny, moving from tadpole to fish to alien space-being (we'd seen him at the twenty-week ultrasound in all his Kubrick-esque weirdness, bigheaded and dreaming of world domination), to the restless, waiting child who liked to practice Tae Bo in my wife's stomach while she tried to paint.

I walked her into the dining area and we looked at all the food. A platter of cheeses, the lasagna, an enormous bowl full of duck and boar sausages, three kinds of mustard, pasta salad, fruit salad, salad salad. I could see into the kitchen, where the caterer was getting ready an enormous chocolate cake.

A commotion began in the other room. A woman shouted. People drew away and the scene revealed itself. The older painter had the younger one in a headlock from behind. "Worthless little shit," he was saying. They moved together that way, the boy's long frame tilted backward and unbalanced, his eyes tight, his red ski hat riding up on his forehead.

"Do you believe this?" I said. "What idiots."

"Post-ironic?" the older one was shouting. "Post-ironic?"

"This is awful," said Tina, alarmed. "Someone needs to stop them."

I figured it might as well be *The Naked Man*. I pushed through a couple of onlookers and quickly reached the two artists. "Hey!" I shouted at the older one. Bill was his name. I think it was Bill. His shirt had little flamingos all over it. Post-ironic, indeed. I pried his hands from around the kid's neck, then got between them and took a deep breath, hoping to inflate myself a size or two so he wouldn't think of messing with me.

"Ha!" shouted Bill, his eyes lit with delight.

"Ha ha," said the kid, behind me, who had dropped to the floor and was now getting to his feet. "Ho ho. Oh, man."

Bill moved past me, and in a moment he and the kid were embracing like teammates who'd each had part of scoring a winning goal. Bill worked the kid's hat around with a muscular hand. "I love this guy," he said.

"When you come to Atlanta," said the kid, "we're going to roast a pig."

We hung around until about ten, me tossing back the wine and helping myself to the food, Tina making polite conversation with more of the guests. She'd gained twenty-five pounds so far, but I'd gained ten, easy. I thought it was the least I could do. That and making encouraging sounds for Frick, my mouth pressed against Tina's belly, something I'd done morning and night after the transfer, back when we were waiting to see if we'd gotten lucky. There were two embryos; only one had managed to hang in, which was what we'd hoped for. Frack had just been there to load the odds, which might sound kind of hard, but these are things you have to be hard about, and twins would have broken the bank for us, although we'd have sucked it up if we'd had to. I made the noises with my lips those first few days, just a quiet pop-popping, like what I imagined bubbles sounded like underwater. I didn't want to upset him, I just wanted him to feel at home. Lately, I sang classic rock and soul to him.

Norma Broccoli walked us to the door. "It's been such a pleasure," she said. "Your work is magnificent. So controlled. Of course the artist herself is just as impressive."

"You're only glad I didn't stage a fistfight," said Tina, smiling.

"Absolutely. Thank you."

Norma looked at me.

"Sorry," I said. "She won't do it. Although, out of curiosity, I wonder how much you might be willing to pay for *The Naked Man*?"

Tina blushed. "We have to go," she said.

"Ten thousand?" I asked.

"You look wonderful," said Norma Broccoli. "Enjoy this time. It's very special."

The walk to the car was cold and silent. "How could you?" she said, when we were inside and I'd started the engine. "Paintings aren't sold that way. You know that."

"Well, maybe they ought to be." I turned on the fan for the heater and put the car into gear and attempted to figure out where the driveway was. We'd parked in a field, and even though there was a net of bright stars glimmering above us, the night was very dark.

"That was crass. You don't talk money to people. Your gallery does that."

"And takes fifty percent."

"They have bills to pay."

"I can't believe you're worrying about your gallery's bills when you don't even have a gallery yet."

"And I can't believe you would embarrass me like that."

"I just wondered. In my world, everyone *knows* what things are worth. A cheap Mexican Stratocaster costs two to three hundred dollars, period. That kid from Atlanta wants eight thousand bucks for a portrait of his girlfriend with a fake black eye? That should fund a couple of pig roasts. I don't know—" I ran over a big rock, making the whole car bounce up and down. "Sorry."

"Just don't strand us out here. We might never be found."

My cell phone rang and I answered it. "Is there a fuse box or something?" Hobey asked.

"Circuit breaker." My fingers were freezing. "In the basement. Bottom of the steps, on the right."

"Thanks!" she said, cheerily.

I pushed "End call." "Circuit breaker," I explained.

"I still don't feel him," said Tina. "It's been hours and hours. It's never this long. He should be awake by now. He should be swimming around."

"Maybe art bores him. Maybe he's meditating." Among the things we knew about Brad was that he practiced transcendental meditation. I'd thought this alone ought to disqualify him, but Tina said she got a feeling from N311. Here were some other things about him. He was five foot ten, an inch taller than me. He'd graduated from an Ivy League school, summa, with a degree in history; I had barely eked out a music degree from a second-rate college in New Jersey. He played soccer, basketball, and tennis, all competitively—I'd never been a team-sports type of guy (Tina claimed that this part of his résumé meant nothing to her, but I wondered if the prospect of reproduction had somehow brought out the latent cheerleader in her). His hair was the same color as mine, which was something. His favorite color was orange. That one had really gotten me. I didn't think I had a favorite color. I liked certain colors at certain times. It seemed unreasonable to ask such a question without any context. But orange? What kind of guy would pick orange? I suspected this answer. It was perhaps the one thing I had on Brad — I was certain he'd lied about his favorite color.

"Hey!" I shouted. "Wake up!"

She put her hand on her belly for a few moments, then looked at me. "Nothing."

"It's OK," I told her. "Really, I'm sure of it. He's come all this way, he's not going to give up now."

"You don't know that," she said. "You don't know anything for certain."

"Did I ever tell you about the mouse? Years ago, back when I lived in Brooklyn, back in my twenties, we had a mouse problem. It was October, and they were coming in to get warm and I was trapping them at the rate of three or four a day. Then one night I hear this weird sound from the next room. I figure out it's a mouse, only it's got a trap on its tail. I mean, there's really nothing wrong with the mouse at all other than fear, but it's got this big Victory-brand trap attached to it slowing it down and making it impossible for it to slip into some nook or crack in the woodwork. My brilliant solution was to try to drown it. I got this forceps we had lying around to use as a roach clip, and I picked the poor guy up by the trap and dunked him into a Chock full o'Nuts can full of water. It was horrible. I still remember every second of it. He struggled in there and even cried out — I'm serious, I heard little mouse screams from inside the can. It must have taken a full minute, or even longer. It seemed like an hour, I know that."

"Why are you telling me this?"

"Because." I watched another departing guest's headlights approach us, momentarily filling our car with light - the side of Tina's face appearing and disappearing before my eyes — then pass away along the driveway. "I'd thought if I just stuck that mouse underwater, he'd turn off — go out like a candle or something. But it's not like that at all. Living things want to live, more than anything. They want to live. It might be the most powerful force in the universe."

She took my hand and gave it a squeeze. "That's a sad story," she said.

At the hotel, there were free cookies out in the lobby, so we took some up to our room and ate them on the bed. She cried a little, but not too much, and I turned on the television to see if they had HBO, which they did, but it was some sex show about middle-aged swingers, and so instead I turned on *TV Land* where there was Andy Griffith. We both thought Barney was one of the great TV characters of all time, and in this particular episode, he was dealing with a station house full of dogs. We'd been talking about getting a dog for Frick, and I said something about that, but she didn't answer. Looking over at her, I realized she'd fallen asleep.

I adjusted her shirt a little — it looked like it was pulling at her around the neck. Then I let my hand rest on her belly. I had no idea who *The Naked Man* was supposed to be, exactly — just some resident of a far-off place where people walked around naked. Someone for Marco Polo to encounter, that's all — an extra. In the painting, my eyes had a nervous quality, and I thought back to how strange I'd felt, standing in the studio of Tina's tiny house, the one she'd sold when we got married, staring at the wall pretending to be naked while she took my photo. I was a lousy actor, even in paint.

"Sugar pie," I whispered. I didn't want to wake Tina up. "Honey bunch. You know that I love you. I can't help myself. I love you and nobody else."

Something inside her — a finger? a foot? — drew a line straight along my palm.

Since I was still dressed, and not tired, I decided to take a little walk. I eased quietly out of the room and down the hall to the elevator. In the lobby, a guy in a business suit was sitting staring into the big, roaring fire in the fireplace like he expected it to talk to him. I pushed open the heavy glass doors. It was still and wet and cold outside. I walked a few blocks toward the center of town, thinking maybe I'd get something else to eat, but then I turned around because I wasn't hungry and I didn't want to get that far away from my family. There was a store directly across from the hotel that had a sign advertising "Typewriter and Calculator Repair." I'd been wanting to look in the window. I was in awe of a business even more hopeless than mine. Calculator repair? There they were, lined up on shelves, maybe ten of them, most with rolls of paper so you could have a printed record of your calculations. There were some typewriters, too. I recognized an IBM Selectric, as well as a couple of Royal Electrics, and even an old Corona portable from the thirties. They had ribbons for sale, little boxes hanging from a display rack. Of course, the world was full of calculators and typewriters, and even if most people never gave them a second thought, it stood to reason that there would be someone out there to look after them, to care about them, to be in charge of their little deaths and resurrections.

BLACK DAYS

Desire had suddenly gone quiet, and the Professor could tell what was coming. They were on the train from Castelpoggio back to Rome, riding facing each other in window seats. She seemed to be working through some deep thought, her eyes narrowed, her fingers pressed together almost as if in prayer.

"What?" he finally asked. Out the window to his left, hedgerows flew by in a blur of greens and browns.

"This train," she said. "I'm getting something."

He looked up through the bars of the luggage rack at their two wheelie bags, hers pink, his black, and his guitar case, which he'd lugged all the way across the ocean for nothing. An announcement came over the intercom, first in Italian, then in English.

"A little girl. I'm feeling her."

"I swear," said the Professor, "it sounds like she's saying the *train god* is in carriage eleven. What the heck do you think a *train god* is?"

"What's the matter? You don't believe in the train god?"

"Not since I was little," said the Professor. He rubbed the back of his neck with his hand. It had gone stiff on the plane on the flight over, and had only gotten worse since then.

"The train god watches over you when you take a train. It's a simple concept."

He tried to smile. Castelpoggio had been a disaster. There had been no Blues Brothers Band, there had been no Les McCann. Instead there had just been the two of them, left to fend for themselves in a hilltop town in Umbria that had no particular attractions. One hotel, two restaurants. Black Days, the festival for which Desire Jones had supposedly been booked as a supporting act, had been canceled months ago. No one had even bothered to tell them.

She was staring at him.

"What little girl?" he asked, wearily.

"On her way to the camps. Down these very tracks."

"Desire," he said. "What are you talking about?"

"World War Two, darling. The murder of sixteen million children."

"It's six million, and the camps were in Germany. And Poland."

"You're wrong," she said. "You don't know your history."

"I *teach* history," he pointed out.

"Taught, don't you mean? I'm surprised they let you." She took a Tucs cracker out of the bag they'd brought with them and ate it. She was in her midfifties, although she'd never told him her age exactly, older than he by nearly twenty years. They'd been playing music together since meeting at a blues jam last September, sleeping together since January, right after he'd come back from his Christmas visit to New Jersey to see his kids, which was also when she'd told him she'd lined up her "European Tour."

"This was a little black girl," she said.

"In Italy? During the war?"

"She got taken away to the camp. Apocalypse."

"Was she from Ethiopia?"

"No, she wasn't from Ethiopia, smart guy. She was from right around here. From Castelpoggio. And they took her by train to Camp Apocalypse." She ate another cracker and swallowed it down with water from a plastic bottle.

The Professor chewed his lip, then took the bottle from her and had a drink himself. It was never clear to him when she was honestly telling him something she thought, and when she was just working to get a reaction out of him. He wasn't even that sure about her singing. Sometimes, when they were on stage at one of the Atlanta bars they played — Nunbetta Barbecue, Blues Station, The Five Spot — he'd hear her voice over the rest of the band, its hard, sharp timbre almost visual to him, like a piece of broken metal poking through the top of a tent. Still, playing with Desire gave him a credibility he'd never enjoyed in any of the all-white blues bands he'd been in. "*Auschwitz*," he said, at last. "Not *Apocalypse*."

"That's what I said."

"No, it isn't. You know it isn't."

"Are you telling me I don't know what I said?"

"I just know what I heard."

"You need to listen better."

"You need to talk better."

"Wait," he said. "I just figured it out. Not *god. Guard*."

She wasn't paying any attention. Sometimes she ignored him totally, as if to make sure he understood that however many degrees he might have, whatever the objective difference between them in terms of achievement and status, she was still the one in charge. Instead, she took out a compact, flipped it open, and examined her eyes.

"*Guard*," he repeated. "There's a *guard* in *carozza* eleven. In case we need him."

"What makes you think the train god is a him?" she asked. "That's sexist."

"You're right. Of course. The train god might just as well be a woman."

But she'd closed her eyes again and wasn't listening. She was psychic. Her mama was, and her grandma, too. She was just changing the subject. He wanted to tell her that it was all right, no one expected her to be sophisticated, to know, for example, what the Via Flaminia was, or to understand much about the Roman Empire. Yesterday, they had hired a driver to take them to see the Roman bridge that was Castelpoggio's only real claim to fame — the Professor had suggested they walk, but the icy stare he earned for that made him regret even trying to be funny — and Desire had barely looked at the thing. "You have to use your imagination," he'd said. "This was a major bridge along one of the most important roads of the ancient world. It's an engineering accomplishment of stunning proportions." He had to admit, he'd found it a bit underwhelming himself, what with the view marred by the smokestacks of some chemical production facility in the background, and the bridge itself little more than a deteriorated arch in the middle of a ravine. Still, he took her lack of participation personally. In the face of what had happened, the embarrassment of coming all this way for nothing, it seemed she could at least try to *appear* to be enjoying herself. Instead, she was punishing him, or trying to. Because, against all reason and evidence, she wanted this whole thing to be his fault.

"This little girl's name was Mary," said Desire.

"Please. Enough."

"You should try to open up your mind. It would do you some good. There's a lot going on that you don't even see or feel." She ate part of another cracker. "It might improve your playing."

"*Mary*, in Italy, would be *Maria*. And the country isn't exactly brimming over with black people, in case you hadn't noticed. There was one camp, I believe, in Trieste. But it would have been for Jews, and it's in the opposite direction."

"Oh," she said. "You own this discussion, huh?"

"You can't just make up stuff about history."

"I know what I know," she said.

He looked at his watch, a recent gift from her, as it happened. Their flight back was tomorrow afternoon. There was just the rest of today to get through, and all of tomorrow morning. He'd been suggesting things to do ever since dinner Friday evening, when they'd sat in the courtyard of the hotel in Castelpoggio trying to make out the menu, trying not to feel like complete fools. The manager, who seemed to comprehend the situation, had comped them appetizers and a bottle of wine. "Black Days," he said. "Was last year very nice, but not so many people. This year — " he waved his hand like a magician making something disappear.

A poster had come in the mail back in February, with The Blues Brothers Band and Les McCann listed right on it, as well as "Special Guests." "That's us," Desire had said, pointing to it. "Special Guests." They would play with a house band, no need to bring a rhythm section. She'd already sent Mr. Tommaso a song list. In Castelpoggio, the first afternoon, the Professor had found the same poster on the side of a building, ripped and weathered and clearly a year old. What had happened? He didn't know. Perhaps one of the headliners had canceled, leaving Mr. Tommaso with no show, just supporting acts. With the exception of their hotel in Rome, Desire had handled all the details — tickets, reservations; she refused to say anything about how or if she was being reimbursed. The Professor suspected the thing had been a scam from the start, with Tommaso collecting money from sponsors and then ducking out. He'd read enough about Italy to know that underneath its shiny modern exterior, corruption was still a simple fact of life.

Desire had spent most of Saturday in the hotel, sulking, while the Professor had gone out walking the steep medieval streets in a light rain. Sunday, they'd had the trip to the bridge. Desire had expressed an interest in shopping, but of course everything was closed. This morning, leaving for the train, she'd gone into a hardware store and spent ten minutes picking up items — a piece of cutlery, a packet of screws — considering them as if appreciating the local art. It had nearly driven the Professor to distraction.

He knew how they'd get through the next twenty-four hours. They would find a wine store, get some carryout goodies — cheeses and sausages and whatnot — and hide themselves away in their hotel room. They could just watch TV. Desire liked television. Perhaps they'd fool around. And then at some point — on the plane, probably — he'd break it to her that things could no longer go on this way. Music was one thing, but the rest of it, the relationship part, that was over.

"I don't know why they'd call something *Black Days* and then go and hire the Blues Brothers anyway," she said.

"I guess it's more the concept of *black*," said the Professor. "Although I think there may be one or two black members of the band. Their music is certainly African American."

"I want to see the skeletons," she said.

"You don't." Ever since she'd noticed the photo in their guidebook of the Capuchin crypt in Rome, with all the bones on display, she'd been claiming interest, but it would be like with the raw oysters. She'd never had one, and kept saying over and over how she wanted to try. So, a few weeks ago, he'd taken her out to a bar that served them. The sight of the plate had clearly disgusted her, but she'd gone ahead anyway and, on his instruction, let one slide down her throat. Instantly, she'd turned ashen and had to run to the bathroom.

"Don't tell me what I do or don't."

"Sorry." He looked around to see if other passengers were paying attention to this. A man with silvery hair and a nice suit made notes in a small, fancy-looking book. A woman was chatting on her cell phone. A boy in a soccer jersey stared sullenly into a magazine.

"And, you need to understand something. *Black* isn't a concept."

"Of course not. I didn't mean it that way. You know that."

"You saw the way people looked at me in Castelpoggio."

He understood she'd felt conspicuous, and perhaps there had been a few stares, but for the most part, it had been his impression that people had treated her like anyone else. It was a small town — of course they were going to stare at strangers. "Well," he said, "they canceled Black Days."

"I am aware of that fact."

"So, people were wondering about you."

"They should wonder," she said.

Two months earlier, in late April, the Professor's Chair had called him into his office to let him know that his one-year contract would not be renewed.

"There were complaints," he said. "I guess you missed a few classes."

"For legitimate reasons. A person can get a cold, you know."

The Chair was a large man, a devotee of barbecue, an expert on Civil War–era munitions, and a devourer of licorice as a substitute for cigarettes. The Professor had always assumed him to be on his side. Collinswood was a small, Christian college; the Professor — whose degree was actually in American Studics — taught three sections of American history to dutiful students who clearly suspected him of something.

"It's pretty well known around the department that you're playing in a band."

"What's wrong with that?"

"Nothing. I'm a music lover myself." He sucked thoughtfully on his Twizzler. He opened department meetings, as required, with a prayer, but the Professor thought he detected at least a degree of irony in his delivery. "I'm sorry," he said. "I've got my marching orders from the dean. But I'm interested. What kind of band is this?"

"Blues," he said. "I'm a guitarist."

He nodded. "You ever heard of Little Luther? My wife and I used to go see him play sometimes. Tiny guy, wears red suits and bolo ties and cowboy boots — very stylish. Skin dark as coffee beans. I mean, like, French roast."

"Nope," said the Professor. "I don't know him."

"We used to see him sometimes at this joint on Piedmont. I thought he was pretty good. Real authentic."

"I'm with Desire Jones," he said.

"I think I've seen that name. Thought it was pronounced the other way. You know, with an accent."

"Nope. No accent."

"Ah," said the Chair.

"So, that's it?"

"I'm afraid so. Yes."

They were both silent. Finally, the Professor put his index finger and thumb to his forehead and brought them forward in a hat-tipping gesture — something he'd never done before in his life — and left the office.

That night, at their gig at Nunbetta Barbecue, he had begun an Etta James song, "Jump into My Fire," which was how they always opened, and Desire had lowered her head and looked at him coldly through her fake eyelashes. She sat back down at a table, leaving him and Scott and T-Man, the bassist and drummer, to play the song as an instrumental. Neither of them seemed surprised — they'd grown used to Desire's moodiness. The Professor went to the microphone and announced, in his best MC voice, *Ladies and gentlemen, let's give it up for Miss Desire Jones!* There were only ten people in the place, but their applause was enough to move her. "I thank you," she said, floating to the front. "My chirruns thanks you. My grandchirruns thanks you. And now, I'd like to sing an old favorite of mine, 'House of the Rising Sun.'"

The Professor felt he was being jabbed slowly with a long knife. He hated the song, and she knew he hated it. He hit the chords with angry, abrupt downstrokes, as if it were a punk anthem, literally punching the tune into submission. He'd had a job, one with a possible future, and he'd blown it for this. He was an idiot. But then, within a few measures, a transformation occurred. His anger and hers seemed to meet and come to some agreement. It was not un-like what happened when they made love, a strange chemistry that never failed to take him by surprise.

"You didn't call me today," she said, at the break. They sat in a red upholstered booth with beers and a basket of peanuts.

"I don't have to call you."

"No," she said. "I guess you don't. But you *could*. Am I right?"

"Desire—"

"Uh-uh-uh-uh. Answer the question. Could you call me?"

"I got fired," he said.

"I don't want to hear about that," she said. "Don't tell me that. What about tenure?"

"Tenure?" he said. "I don't have tenure."

"Well, maybe you should look into it."

He cracked a peanut open one-handed. "You're right," he said. "I'll look into it."

Their hotel in Rome was the same one they'd stayed at after arriving, Albergo Rosso, near the Campo dei Fiori, and it hadn't gotten any nicer while they were away. The Professor had found it for them on the Internet, where it looked just fine, centrally located, all that. But the place was run down, the reception staff rude. This was his fail-ure, and Desire had made sure to let him know about it, pretending not to hear when he said things, staring off into space. There was a lounge on the second floor with an upright piano and some dingy furniture, its walls decorated with black-and-white photographs of the Forum, the Coliseum, Trajan's column.

"I have the strangest feeling I've been here before," she said when they were checked into their new room.

"Uncanny," he said, opening the shutters and looking down. In the piazza below, there were two bars. One had tables set out, but at the moment only one person sat at one, a woman in a sun hat drinking a glass of something.

"I'm hungry," she said. "I hate this Italian food." She looked at herself in the gold-flecked mirror, picking at something in her eye. "Worst pizza I've had in my life."

"You have to stop comparing it to the U.S. It's a different concept."

"I don't care for the concept." She put on her down-home voice. "I want me a plate of ribs. Fried chicken and potato salad."

"We can find that. An 'American'-themed place with a plaster statue of George Bush outside wearing a lone star apron and holding a barbecue fork."

"That sounds better to me than another plate of spaceship, or whatever you call that stuff we had last night."

"Rocket. Arugula. It's not really that exotic. Even my boys eat it."

"How do you know what they eat?"

"Don't try to get to me about them, all right? I'm good with them."

"They think you're like Batman, huh? Teacher in the day, and then you put on your personamus at night and become Captain Guitar."

"My what?"

"Personamus. Just like I'm *Desire*. That's my personamus. You've got one. Everyone's got one."

"Where do you think the guitar would be safer?" he asked. "In the closet or under the bed?"

"Closet. You don't think that's a word?"

"I didn't say that."

"You don't say a lot of things." She went and closed the shutters again. "Come on. I want to eat, and then I want to see some dead people."

They took a cab to the Capuchin crypt. "You're going to hate this," the Professor told her as he paid the driver from his dwindling funds.

"Please stop telling me what you think I think."

The admission fee was five euros each. They followed the crowd in to the series of rooms, each decorated in a different way with bones. Entire bodies were on display, still in their robes, faces remarkably human still, although desiccated and ghoulish, the eyes still seeming to stare despite the absence of eyeballs. They admired a chandelier made out of bones. There were altars made of piles of skulls. The Professor wanted to make a joke, but couldn't think of anything. The group of tourists they were moving through the place with was mostly silent, except for the occasional gasp of disbelief.

He stood behind her as she examined the reclining body of a monk in his cell. Without saying anything, he backed up, letting a young couple — Germans, from the look of them — take his place. It would be so easy just to leave her here. He imagined the afternoon he might have on his own, unencumbered by her. Perhaps he'd visit a museum, or some churches. Or maybe just find a place to sit and drink espresso and look out at the people passing by. Rome was full of fashionable, beautiful women. Why did he have to be stuck taking care of someone who worked at a bank, ate too many doughnuts, and was on a first-name basis with the stars of any number of reality television shows?

Desire turned around looking for him, then came over. "You scared?" she whispered.

"Are you?"

She shook her head, but her face had lost some color, and he knew she wasn't handling it well. "It's awful," she said. "Why would anyone do this?"

"They saw death differently. We're too influenced by horror movies." Still, he felt it too. It was one thing to look at a single skeleton, quite another to see an entire chandelier made of scapulae.

"I need to get out of here," said Desire.

"There's more," he said. "Come on."

"I'm serious. We have to go."

"What did I tell you?" asked the Professor, and followed her retreating form out past the guard, to whom he gave a pleasant *grazie*. He stopped to buy a couple of postcards for the boys, then proceeded out onto the Via Veneto.

When he got outside, he found her leaning against the wall of the building, her eyes obscured by her big sunglasses. "Desire?" he said.

"Oh, my god," she said.

"Just outside the original city boundaries are the catacombs. Probably two million bodies buried there."

"I don't want to hear it, all right? Please, just take me home."

Back at the hotel, they took naps on separate beds. He awoke to the sounds of her in the shower, so he sat in the chair by the window and went through the various restaurant recommendations in his guidebook, many of which he'd read aloud to Desire at least twice already.

She emerged fully dressed from the tiny bathroom. When they had sex it was always with the lights off. She might not have been beautiful, but he loved the feel of her, the surprising muscularity of her thighs and calves, the delicate lavender smell of her skin.

"Something's not right with that shower," she said, adjusting her metallic gold blouse. "Or the toilet, neither."

"We can go across the river," he suggested. "The book says there are lots of restaurants in Trastevere."

She turned away. He approached, reaching around, pressing himself up against her. She made a tiny sound, an intake of breath combined with what he took to be a moan, and understanding this as surrender, he moved closer. She put her hands down on the writing desk by the wall, her head dipped toward the informational brochures spread across it. Then she spun around and slapped him hard on the mouth.

"What the hell?" he said. "What's the matter?"

"You know what's the matter."

"I do?" He wondered if it were possible she could have somehow seen into him. He was pretty sure his lip was bleeding.

"Say it."

"Say what?"

"You think I'm stupid. What else would I be? But I'm not." She took another swing at him, but this time he saw it coming and ducked out of the way.

"Whoa there," he said, probing his lip with his tongue.

She came at him, and it was so unexpected that she took him backward into a chair, which fell over, tangling his legs and causing him to fall as well. He rolled toward the center of the room to get clear, then jumped to his feet. "Hey!" he shouted. "You could have really hurt me!"

"Come on," she said. "Fight back like a man." She flailed with her hands in the direction of his face, and he put up his own hands to defend himself, and then, unsure what else to do, threw a punch in her direction that bounced harmlessly off her forearm. She was still moving forward, still trying to hit him. He grabbed her by her wrists, which worked for a few seconds, but then she bit his arm, so he had to let go. She then landed a roundhouse right to the side of his head. When he recovered his balance he charged her and grabbed her around the throat in a choke hold.

"You have to calm down," he said. "You have to calm down." Her eyes were moist and full of hatred. "You. Have. To. Calm. Down." Slowly, he released the pressure. Neither one of them did anything at all. He watched a spider bungee jump out of the high corner of the ceiling, then make its way quickly back up into the shadows.

"Desire?"

"All right," she said, at length. "I'm calm."

It was loud in the square, with the mingled sounds of voices and laughter and music spilling out of the bar across the street. Their tablecloth was red and white checked, their waiter obsequious, yet obviously dismissive of yet another couple of American tourists. Neither of them had said a thing about what had happened.

A middle-aged man with an accordion, accompanied by a younger man who had a violin, set up a few yards away from their table and proceeded to play a medley of gypsy-sounding music. When they were done, Desire waved them over and gave them five euros.

"Thank you, thank you, beautiful lady," said the older one, who was clearly in charge. The other simply bowed.

"You are *too* kind," said Desire, her personamus swinging into play.

"American?" asked the accordionist, pleased to report the obvious. "On holiday?"

"I'm here professionally," said Desire. "You may have heard of Black Days? In Castelpoggio?"

They looked at each other briefly, and the younger one said a few words in Italian that seemed to trigger something for the other, who the Professor had now come to see was certainly his father. They had the same eyes, the same heavy brow, the same aquiline nose. "Yes, yes," he said. "Of course."

"Well, I'm one of the black people. Desire Jones," she said. "From Atlanta, Georgia."

"Atlanta!" he repeated. "Very nice! You are a singer?"

"*Si*," said Desire. "*Bravo*." The Professor massaged his forehead. Within moments, he was alone at the table, watching Desire confer with them on what they could play that she might sing. There were another eight tables besides theirs, two of them unoccupied. Perhaps a dozen people, total.

"I'd like to do a little blues number for you," she said, stepping forward in front of the two men. "Accompanied by my new friends, Matteo and Giorgio." The older man played a quick flourish of notes on his accordion.

And then she was singing it again, "House." In this context, with its rudimentary melody underlain by the wheezy, French-café-in-the-fifties sound of the accordion, the song was even more painful to him. Plus, the violinist kept doubling Desire's vocal at the same pitch. *Bad idea*, he wanted to tell him. *No one sounds good that way.* The two men flanked her, one on either side, smiling at him, at the other diners at their tables respectfully enduring this interruption. They formed a strange sort of family portrait.

He pulled forty euros from his wallet and tucked the bills under his water glass, then stood. Her eyes met his — they simply acknowledged him. For three days he'd been longing to say to her, *If you're so damned psychic, what the hell are we doing in Italy at all?* Then he walked away.

At the statue of Giordano Bruno in the middle of the square, he observed a group of young people standing around smoking and laughing and wondered if they understood that they were at a place of execution, that the man on the platform above them had been burned alive there. He was just getting ready to ask one of them for a cigarette — he was doing his best to figure out how he might say this in Italian — when, like birds, they moved as a group, suddenly, all in one direction. He watched them go. They were headed back in the direction from which he'd come, and looking that way, he realized that a little audience had begun to form near Desire and the two musicians. She was singing something else now, and although he'd put quite a bit of distance between them, her voice carried enough that it was audible over the din of the crowded square. The song was

Marvin Gaye's "I Heard It Through the Grapevine." It was one they'd practiced in preparation for Black Days, the two of them sitting for hours going over it and over it in the living room of her apartment in Marietta that always smelled of fried fish and potpourri. That living room, too, was the first place they'd been naked together, with just the blue-gray light from the parking lot outside filtering through the Venetian blinds to see by, her small Christmas tree still set up alongside the television. And it was where she'd finally told him her real name, Janice, whispered it tentatively in his ear like a password, before they'd put their clothes back on and stepped out into the cold, early morning to see about getting something to eat.

THE FLANNERY O'CONNOR AWARD FOR SHORT FICTION